HEX AFTER DARK

M.J. CAAN

VINCI
BOOKS

By M.J. Caan

Singing Falls Witches

Thank you to my readers for making all of this possible.
And especially thank you, B. You're the best.

Vinci Books

vinci-books.com

Published by Vinci Books Ltd in 2025

1

A CIP catalogue record for this book is available from the British Library.
Paperback ISBN: 9781036705640
The EU GPSR authorised representative is Logos Europe, 9 rue Nicolas Poussion, 17000 La Rochelle, France contact@logoseurope.eu

Printed and bound in Great Britain by Clays Ltd, Elcograf S.p.A.

Chapter One

Trudging through two inches of muck that threatened to pull her shoes off was not how Torie Bliss had envisioned her evening going. She frowned at her best friend Jasmin's back as they made their way through the lowland bog, the moonlight glinting off the metal of her gardening tools. "Let's go harvest some plants, they said...it will be fun, they said," Torie grunted. "And in case it wasn't clear, you are the *they* that said this."

Jasmin waved her hand over her shoulder. "Yeah, yeah, so I've heard. But you didn't exactly protest too much when I brought the idea up." She stopped, hands on hips, as she gulped some deep breaths. "As a matter of fact, if I remember right, you said there was no better time than the present to make it happen."

They were out in the middle of the night, on a steep hillside leading to a plateau where a very specific plant grew. It was one they needed for a very specific spell they had discovered in one of Torie's mother's grimoires.

Torie frowned. "Yes, well that was before I knew it was

going to cost me my favorite pair of hiking boots. I'll never get all this mud off them."

"Well, what is the point of having them if you're not actually going to wear them?"

Torie blinked rapidly at her friend. "I wear them. Just not out in the mud and dirt. They're too nice for all that."

Jasmin chuckled, took a deep breath, and started moving forward again. "Come on, we have to find that lunarwort. It only blooms under a full moon and we only have two hours before it's gone."

Torie sighed and followed her friend, her boots squelching in the mud. She looked up at the moon, a giant orb in the night sky, and said a silent prayer that they would find what they were looking for.

"And what kind of plant only blooms for a couple of hours a night, once a month? Who came up with that?" she mumbled.

"A magic one, obviously," answered Jasmin as they crested the hill, coming to an open field before them.

The light of the full moon broke across the open space like a shimmering silver carpet. There was very little wind to disturb the growth, and the stillness of the stems of the reeds and large grasses only added to the feeling of serenity the two witches could only admire in awe.

"Alright," said Jasmin. "The lunarwort should be growing on the other side of this field. We should have about an hour to harvest some before it goes dormant for another month."

Torie nodded and followed her friend, their eyes scanning the expanse before them for the telltale glimmer of the plant. Somewhere in the distance, or maybe it came from behind them, an owl hooted, followed by the sound of large, ruffled wings disturbing the silence. Torie started, looking over her shoulder then up at the star-filled sky.

"That was an owl, Torie," said Jasmin. She hadn't even bothered to look back at her friend.

"What kind of owl is that big? Who knows what that could have been."

"Barn owls can have a wingspan of up to four feet." Jasmin stopped and turned to her friend, a twinkle in her eyes. "Or it could have been an owl-shifter. Who knows how big those can get."

Torie swallowed hard, her eyes darted to and fro.

Jasmin laughed softly as they continued. "Oh, calm down. Why are you so jumpy? You've fought vampires, golems and all manner of demons before. But now you're afraid of an owl?"

Torie huffed. "I'm not afraid. I just don't like being out here in the dark. It's so wide open and we are exposed. Anything could attack us, plus, we can't see in the dark."

"Hah. It's nighttime, but it's not dark out. There is a difference. Not a cloud in the sky to obscure the moonlight. And besides, we have this." She held out one hand and produced a ball of shimmering, blue magic that bounced across the field before disappearing in a soft pop of iridescent fireworks.

Torie felt a tingle in the back of her head, a pulling sensation that tickled just under her scalp.

"Wait, Jasmin, do that again."

Her friend gave her a questioning look, but did as she asked, producing another ball of magic and sending it sailing across the field.

There was definitely a reaction this time. Torie wasn't sure where it came from, or what it was, and she looked around puzzled.

"What is it?" asked Jasmin.

"I'm not sure. Didn't you feel that? Something reacted to your magic. It was like a whisper that I felt, instead of heard."

Jasmin looked around, studying the field and the tree line on the far side. She sent her senses outward, feeling for anything that could account for the type of disturbance Torie was feeling. "I don't feel anything."

"It's gone now. It was only there when you sent your magic out."

Jasmin squinted in the distance. "It could have just been the area itself, responding to magical energy. This area is known to collect and hold power. That's why the lunarwort grows here, and only here. The soil is rich with primal energies. Witches have been coming here for generations to practice moon magic."

Torie smiled. "Good old Singing Falls. A surprise in every nook and corner."

They continued, and as they reached the far side of the field, they got their first look at the mystic plant for which they had undertaken a mile's-long hike in the middle of the night.

"And that," said Jasmin, pointing, "is what we came for."

There, before the field ended and broke into the line of pine trees where the forest started, were the most beautiful plants Torie had ever seen. The lunarwort was a small, delicate flower, growing to a height of about five inches, with a petite white blossom and slender green stem. Its petals were dusted with a silvery, moonlight sheen, and the center of the flower was illuminated with a brilliant golden hue. Torie thought she detected a gentle, ethereal fragrance carried in the air around it, like a soft whisper of enchantment. The leaves curved gracefully, reaching upward to the sky in clusters. Moonlight bathed them and caused a rippling effect to pass through the leaves in a light show that drew the witches' eyes. The closer Torie and Jasmin stepped to them, the more the flowers shimmered in response.

"So pretty," Torie said. "It's almost a shame to pick them." She looked over at her friend, who seemed to be studying the ground around the flowers with a frown. "What's wrong?"

Jasmin placed a hand on her chin in thought. "I'm not sure. They don't look quite right. They should be taller and growing much closer together. As a matter of fact, there should be many more of them. Half of the field should be covered in them, not just this one section."

"Are they affected by temperature extremes or anything like that? It's been unseasonably cold the last couple of weeks," Torie said.

Jasmin shook her head. "No. Lunarwort thrives on magic. The weather has no effect on them at all." She reached out a glowing hand, holding it towards the plants. In response, they stretched in her direction, their shimmer turning into a lightship of glittering beauty. "They seem fine, however. Maybe I'm just remembering them wrong. It's been years since I've been up here during a full moon." She shrugged. "We don't have long, so time to harvest."

"And you're sure removing them from the ground won't hurt them?"

"They will be fine. In another hour they will recede back into the earth, recharging, and waiting to spring forth again next month. The blossoms are filled with the power we need for the spell. Once we harvest them, the energy will go dormant, until it's mixed with the rest of the ingredients called for."

She reached for her gardening shears and trowel, handing the tiny shovel to Torie.

"Loosen the earth around them and then pull the plant free root and all. Try not to damage the stalk. Unlike most plants, removing the root is what allows new ones to grow in their place."

They set about harvesting the plant, taking care not to damage the delicate leaves. Jasmin began to hum slightly as they gathered the flowers and placed them in the cloth satchels each carried.

Torie smiled as the flowers pulsed in cadence with Jasmin's voice. "You really do have a way with plants. I wish I had your green thumb—" She stopped, her body stiffening.

Jasmin stopped humming. "Are you feeling it again?"

Torie nodded. "For just a second, yes. But it was stronger that time." She stood, adjusting her satchel. "It's definitely coming from...there." She pointed to an area to their right where a patch of the field faded away before leading into a section of bushy overgrowth just before the tree line began. "I may not have your way with plants, but something is off about the ground in that direction."

"Agreed," said Jasmin. "I can feel it now as well. Come on."

Together, they moved cautiously in the direction Torie had indicated. They stopped when they reached an area of heavy overgrowth. The vines and vegetation had intertwined aggressively, interweaving with roots of all kinds.

"This looks natural...but at the same time unnatural," said Jasmin. She closed her eyes and held out her hands as she began to chant.

"Let the plants of this place lift the veil of secrecy,

so the truth may be revealed and made known to me."

In response, the ground heaved, and the vegetation shivered before drawing back and separating. The earth roiled and opened as it pushed a body upward into view.

Torie gasped, one hand over her mouth as they drew back.

Even with the face turned away from them, they could tell from the size and the clothing that it was the body of a man, slight of build. Dirt and moss were caked over it, and several centipedes and ants scurried away from the corpse.

"Holy mother! Who would do this?" demanded Torie.

Despite her trepidation, Jasmin peered closer. "This hasn't been here very long. And there are no signs of digging tools where the earth would have been broken to dig a grave." She stood back, staring at her friend, eyes wide. "You know what that means?"

Torie nodded, still not wanting to look at the body. "Magic?"

"Yep. Someone killed him, and then had the ground swallow him up like this. I'm betting that's the disturbance you were sensing."

Torie let out a sigh as she fished her cell phone from one of the pockets of her satchel. "Just once. Just once, I'd like to go for a hike, walk around a corner, walk out of a store...anything; and not run into something horrific."

Jasmin snorted. "You're in the wrong town for that. Calling Max?"

Torie nodded. The town sheriff, who happened to be a werewolf and the best friend of her boyfriend, was going to love this one.

"Might as well tell him to get Emil up here as well. Something tells me he's going to be needed."

Dr. Emil Faun was the resident medical examiner, and sprite, for the county. Unlike Max, he would undoubtedly be excited at the sight of a murder scene like this.

"Is that because you're looking for a reason to see him again?" Torie chided with a smile.

Jasmin averted her eyes, thankful that moonlight would obscure any signs of discomfort. "Just trying to make both their lives easier by getting them here at the same time. While you do that, I'm going to nose around. See if I can find any magical residue that might give us a clue as to what happened."

Torie nodded; her attention captured by the gruff voice on the other end.

"It's the middle of the night and you're calling me. What foulness have you uncovered now?" said Max, his voice filled with sleepiness and annoyance.

"Oh, you hit that one right on the head," Torie said with a sigh.

Chapter Two

As expected, Max was in a foul mood, but was also laser focused on everything about the crime scene. His enhanced senses could only pick up the scents of Torie, Jasmin, and the deceased. No sign of whoever had committed the crime. That was in keeping with what Jasmin's magic had told her as well. There was no trace of anyone else being in the area.

Max was crouched down next to the body while furiously scribbling in his notepad as Torie moved to stand next to him.

"Any ideas?" she asked.

He looked up at her and frowned. "Yes. I think you two are magnets for the weird and macabre. Why is it that you are always stumbling onto scenes like this?" I opened my mouth to speak but he held up a hand. "That was rhetorical."

Torie pursed her lips and watched the big sheriff as he studied the body. "Where's Emil?"

"He's on his way. Should be here any minute now," Max answered.

Then, as if on cue, the little sprite emerged from the woods, taking the small group by surprise.

"Doc, where did you come from?" asked Max, his eyes darting to the darkness behind the medical examiner.

Emil Faun frowned, almost as if he didn't understand the question. "From my house of course. You called me, after all."

Max blinked at him. "No, I mean just now. The road is that way—" he motioned behind him with his thumb, "—yet you came out of the—you know what? Never mind. Here's the body, start doing whatever it is you do."

"Hi, Emil." Jasmin had popped up and was standing next to the examiner with her hands clasped behind her back.

His smile reached all the way to his eyes as he nodded. "Hello, Jasmin. It's good to see you." The reason for him to be there seemed to come flooding back to him when Max cleared his throat. "Oh, um...yes. The body. Who found it?"

"We did," said Jasmin, eagerly. "I can tell you whatever you need to know about it."

Max rolled his eyes. "And while you're doing that, I'm going to walk the perimeter. See if I can pick up anything further out."

"I'll go with you," Torie said.

The big wolf grumbled but nodded. Together, they headed off towards the tree line, crossing into the shadowed darkness created by the canopy of growth above them.

"What were you two doing up here anyway?" Max said, walking slowly through the thickets.

"We were harvesting lunarwort. It's a plant that only grows here in the light of the full moon. We're casting a spell I found and it's one of the ingredients."

Max was silent as he surveyed the ground, moving

forward slowly. His body was tense, and Torie could tell he was using all his senses as he swept his gaze across the forest floor.

"Would some light help?" she asked, holding up a hand to create a glowing ball of orangish light.

Max shook his head. "Thanks, but no. I can see perfectly fine in the dark, and the shadows created by your magic are...not natural. It throws off my senses."

Recalling her light, Torie walked on behind him in silence. A branch cracking caused her to jump slightly, and Max turned to her.

"I know," she said, "There's nothing to be afraid of out here that I can't handle."

"Well, true, but that's not what I was going to say. I was going to say that it was just a deer stepping on some twigs to our right while foraging. Nothing more."

Torie took in a deep breath, drawing in the scent of dry pine needles and the musty odor of decaying leaves. She felt comfortable with Max and was thankful for his presence, even if he was grumpy.

He stopped short, squatting down to run his hands over the earth in front of them. He picked up a bit of dirt and sniffed at it.

"What is it?" asked Torie.

He sniffed again before cocking his head to one side, listening intently. "Someone was just here."

And then Torie felt it; the same tickling at the back of her head that she experienced when she and Jasmin were crossing the field. She spun around, and this time cast a swath of magic, a spell designed to illuminate areas hidden by incantation.

The shrubbery behind them rippled and shrank back from her power. Immediately, Max was in wolf form and pounced into the undergrowth, Torie fast on his heels. She could feel whatever had been watching them in retreat, disappearing through the dense foliage at a rapid pace. She tried to cast her thoughts ahead, see if she could get a look at whoever—or whatever—it might have been. But whatever it was, it was bathed in magic that she wasn't familiar with, and it shrugged off her attempts to grasp it with her power.

"Max! It's shifted direction—turned left!" she called to her friend.

With preternatural agility, the big wolf stopped mid-stride and leapt to his left, the woods shaking with the force of his stride as he ran. He quickly pulled away from Torie as she struggled to draw in enough breath to flood her struggling lungs with oxygen. She was so focused on the being they were chasing that she nearly ran into Max's backside when she burst free of the brush.

The wolf had stopped in a small clearing that looked like a game trail and was sniffing the ground heavily.

"Do you still sense them?" he said to her through the mental rapport she shared with all shifters in their non-human form.

She closed her eyes and reached outward, probing the surrounding region. Nothing.

"No," she said, opening her eyes. "Whatever it was, it's just...gone."

Max shimmered in place as he shifted back into his human form. "How can that be? What kind of magic are we facing?"

"No idea. But we better get back to the others. Make sure this wasn't just to draw us away."

Max nodded and they hurried through the woods, Torie trusting Max's unerring senses to guide them back to the crime scene. Both Jasmin and Dr. Faun looked up from studying the body and knew immediately that something was wrong.

"What happened?" said Jasmin, not bothering to mask any concerns she felt for her friend. "Are you okay?"

Torie waved, letting her know they were fine, as she bent over, gathering breath into her still-aching lungs.

"We found signs of someone, or something, watching us from in the woods," said Max. "We tried to chase it down, but it escaped."

Jasmin frowned, her eyes flicking from one to the other. "Do you think it was whoever was responsible for this?" She gestured to the body behind her.

"No idea," said Torie. "But they were definitely magical. Nothing human moves the way this thing did." She glanced at the medical examiner. "Do you believe this was a murder?"

"And if it was a murder, was it committed here or was this just where the body was dumped?" added Max.

"Both excellent questions," said Emil. "And ones that I will have answers to once the body is back at my lab so I can examine it closer. I did find something of interest, but I'd rather not say for certain what it is until I can run a couple of tests. I can say that the body has only been here for a couple of hours before being found."

Torie nodded. "So more likely than not, whatever that was in the woods was either involved or saw what happened."

"Agreed," said Max. "For now, let's get this body back to Dr. Faun's office. I'll come back in the morning with Elric and scout the area farther north of where the trail went cold. See if we can't pick something up."

Jasmin turned to Torie. "Speaking of your man, where is Elric?"

"He was going to run some errands in town earlier tonight and then spend the evening at his place cleaning it up. He's making sure he gets that security deposit back," Torie answered.

Jasmin's eyes lit up. "Oh, that's right. This weekend is the big day. You guys are moving in together." She wiggled her eyebrows lasciviously.

In response, Torie rolled her eyes. "Yes, we will officially be living in sin."

Jasmin smiled. "Please. You know how happy I am for you both. I just can't wait to see how that works out. A witch, a werewolf and a dragon living together in an enchanted house. How fun."

"Might as well be two witches," said Max, "Considering the fact you live right next door to them and are over at Torie's house most of the time."

Jasmin laughed. "Oh, you know I'll be sitting on my porch with a big bowl of popcorn watching it all."

"Ha ha," Torie deadpanned. "Come on, we better get going if we're going to get these lunarworts under cover before daylight breaks."

"Do you need a lift?" asked Max. "Cos otherwise, I'll stay here with the good doc until the medic team can get here to transport the body downtown."

"No, we're fine," said Jasmin as they moved away from the medical examiner. "We're parked just off the main road. It's a straight hike back down for us. You keep an eye on Emil." Her voice dropped until it was barely above a whisper. "If something capable of eluding the two of you is prowling around up here, I don't think he should be left alone."

"Agreed," whispered Torie.

They turned to leave and waved goodbye to Emil. He popped his head up and waved enthusiastically back.

"And thank you for the concern, Jasmin. But I assure you, I can take care of myself." He smiled, and then returned to collecting bits of dirt and placing it carefully in plastic baggies.

"Darned sprite hearing," said Jasmin, shaking her head as they marched off.

They made the descent back to Jasmin's SUV in silence. Once at the car, Torie turned to her friend. "Whatever that was that Max and I chased, is the same thing I sensed watching us as we were trekking through that field."

Jasmin nodded. "Figured as much. But why didn't it attack? Why just watch us? Especially knowing we were more likely than not going to stumble across that body." She unlocked the doors, and they climbed inside.

"No idea," said Torie. "Unless it wanted us to find the body."

"Yeah. That's what I was afraid of."

The night sky was split by a bolt of lightning in the distance, and from habit, Torie counted the seconds until the rumble of thunder hit them.

"Looks like there is a storm coming. With luck, we can get home before the rain," she said.

Jasmin stared out the front window looking up at the sky. "I hope Emil gets everything he needs from the site. It looks like it's going to pour. That will completely wash away any evidence he doesn't collect."

She started the big car's engine and eased out onto the main road that would take them back to their houses just outside of town.

Torie sat silently, staring out the passenger side window.

Her thoughts were on the body they found. Neither of them had recognized the man. He hadn't been dressed for night weather, and certainly didn't appear to have hiked the ridge the way she and Jasmin had. She flashed back to the way the man was bound by the earth, his mouth slightly open and filled with dirt and rotted vegetation. Whoever he was, he deserved better than being consigned to the ground in such a manner.

No matter what Emil's reports were going to say, she was sure of one thing. Someone had killed him up on that mountain. And she was now determined to find out who.

Chapter Three

"Come on, I'll show you how to prepare these," Jasmin said, as she threw the car into park outside Torie's house.

They climbed the couple of steps to the large, welcoming front porch leading to double glass doors. Torie reached out with her mind, feeling for the wards protecting her home. Confident they were undisturbed, she dropped them and pushed the door open.

As soon as the stepped into the foyer, Leo came bounding down the hall to greet them. A flap of his leathery wings sent the little dragon airborne and into Torie's arms where he nuzzled his snout against her chest. She ran a hand along the ridge of his head, cooing to him.

"Hello, little one. How's my happy baby tonight? Did you miss me?"

In response the little dragon rested his head against her and let out a puff of smoke that circled Torie's face. She laughed, waving her hand to clear the air. "And here's Auntie Jazzy...she missed you as well."

The dragon flitted from Torie's arms to Jasmin's. She

grunted as he climbed her chest to land on her shoulder, wrapping his tail lovingly around her neck.

"Okay, okay," Jasmin said playfully. "I don't need to go home smelling like a chimney. Go play." She placed the little guy on the floor and watched as he scampered off towards the back of the house where Torie's study was. "He's definitely growing. What are you going to do when he reaches maturity?"

Torie sighed. "I suppose I'll have to build him something bigger out back."

"That's not what I meant. He's a dragon, Torie."

"I know. But...he's my baby. I'll deal with it at some point. But not just yet."

Together, they walked through the spacious kitchen and out the patio doors. It was just starting to rain lightly as they made their way to the greenhouse Torie had built off to one side of the main house. Once inside, they plopped their satchels on the wooden worktable in the center of the space. The warm, humid air was heavy with the sweet scent of blooming flowers and the earthy aroma of fresh potting soil.

Jasmin took in a deep breath. "I love this place. You really outdid yourself."

"Well, I couldn't have done it without you. You've probably forgotten more about plants than I'll ever know."

Jasmin smiled as she took out the lunarwort she had collected and placed it on the table. "And don't you forget it."

Torie placed her own plants next to those of her friend, marveling at the fact that they still looked as fresh as they had when glowing under the moonlight. "Now what?"

"Their power is in the leaves, but they need to be dried just right in order not to let the mystical energies leak out. We need to use a spell that is a combination of healing and thanks, and then hang them upside down on a pegboard made of white oak."

Torie moved to one of the floor-to-ceiling cabinets built into the shed and opened it, retrieving a hardwood board with several holes cut into it.

"Got it," she said, bringing it to the worktable.

"And now, we bind it in place with enchanted spider silk."

Again, Torie shuffled off to the cabinet and retrieved a small wooden box painted red. Inside, she found a spool of gossamer thread that sparkled silver at her touch. She laid it before them on the table and watched as Jasmin picked up a length and wrapped it around the stem of one of the plants. She nodded to Torie to mimic her actions as she secured the plant, leaves down, on the pegboard. As she did, she began to speak.

"I thank you, sister plants, for your service and aide,
may you be entombed in magic, free from harm and dismay."

Torie repeated the incantation and mirrored her friend's actions until all the lunarwort was strung up on the board. Then, Jasmin took the board and stood it up on one end of the table, leaning back against the wall.

"That's pretty much it," she said.

"Now what?" asked Torie.

"Now, we wait. It will take a few days before the leaves are at the right degree of dryness to grind into the powder to create the potion for the spell."

"Good to know. But can I just ask one thing? In light of the tragedy we just uncovered, is now really the best time to be playing around with spells we've never tried before? I mean...I know Max didn't mean anything by it, but he has a point. This type of stuff seems drawn to us. What if experimenting with new spells just amplifies whatever is going on around here?"

She followed Jasmin to the large copper sink at one end of the greenhouse and waited for her friend to wash up before she ran her own hands under the warm water.

Jasmin dried her hands and turned to face Torie. "This is how we learn. How we get better. We have an obligation to this town and this community. We can't just sit back on our laurels and hope we will always be good enough to take on what's always waiting around the next corner. Our enemies aren't waiting. You think whoever or whatever did that to that man on the mountain is sitting back thinking they've done enough? We both know that's not the case. We have to continually grow...otherwise, we're just sitting ducks for the next big bad that comes for us or our loved ones."

Her words hung in the air, waiting to be absorbed. Finally, Torie nodded. "You're right, of course. I just can't help but wonder if all this would be happening if I had never showed up in this town."

Jasmin took both of her friend's hands in hers and stared her in the eye. "Torie, as powerful as we may be, neither of us can answer a question like that. But what I can say is that I would not change a thing that has happened since you came into my life. Because meeting you has been one of my life's greatest joys. You are my best friend, and the sister I would have chosen. I will never question why you're here; I'm just going to be thankful that you are."

Torie meshed her lips tightly as tears threatened to overwhelm her. "Oh stop. You're going to make me cry, and no one wants to see that."

Jasmin pursed her lips. "Yeah, you got that right. You keep that to yourself."

Torie laughed and pulled her friend in for a quick hug. "And right back at you."

They parted and Jasmin let out a sharp exhale. "Alright, I say we try to get whatever sleep we can, then meet and head to town. We can go the bakery as soon as it opens and see how Fionna is doing. She hired those two associates and wants us to meet them."

Torie glanced at her watch, feeling the tug between being at the house when Elric returned and being there for Fionna. Although Torie, Jasmin, and Fionna had worked hard to make the bakery successful, she wasn't sure how well it would be received. It was especially popular with the breakfast crowd, but Torie was uncertain as to just how much community support there would be. She was torn between wanting to be there for Elric and wanting to know how the bakery would do.

"I'll meet you back at the car in thirty minutes. We can't leave our girl hanging."

Torie opened the door to the bakery and was immediately faced with a large man's back. The line to order stretched from the counter to the doors, with more than a few people curved around to the side, giving the two witches a hard stare in case they thought they were going to break the line.

"Oh wow," said Jasmin. "I knew it would be a hit, but this...Now I kind of wish we had waited on the lunarwort and been here for the opening instead."

It was indeed beyond their expectations. As silent partners, they had agreed to take part in any financial decisions, the menu and the decor of the bakery, but the day-to-day management would fall to Fionna. The squirrel shifter had worked tirelessly, and through the setback of finding a dead body on site, to meet the opening day deadline.

Scanning the shop, Torie and Jasmin saw their friend flitting from seating area to seating area, greeting customers, offering coffee refills and chatting amicably. As busy as she was, she had an ear-to-ear smile that couldn't be hidden.

"Someone's in their glory," said Jasmin.

Torie nodded. "I can't remember when I've seen her this happy before." She swept her gaze to the front counter where there was a young woman smiling and taking orders while a male worked feverishly behind her, bustling in and out of the swinging doors that led to the prep kitchen. "Look there." Torie nudged Jasmin and pointed with her chin.

"Well, I'll be. Come on," said Jasmin as she and Torie walked around the counter and back to the serving area, to come up behind Glen.

"Well, well. How did your wife rope you into this?" asked Torie.

Glen spun around to face the women, blowing a long strand of hair that had managed to escape her hairnet, out of her face.

"Torie, Jasmin," she said, her voice exasperated. "Thank goodness you're here! This place is crazy. I came by earlier to wish Fionna a happy first day, and it was just swamped. She threw a hairnet and apron at me and told me to start filling pastry orders. I don't have a clue what I'm doing."

Jasmin laughed and disappeared into the back before returning with matching aprons and nets, handing one set to Torie. Together, they started greeting patrons and assisting Glen to fill orders for pastries and coffee.

After a bit, Torie turned to her friend. "You got this? I'm

going to go help the kid in the back with the kitchen orders. Looks like he's getting a bit behind."

Jasmin nodded, and she was off, walking through the swinging doors and right into the doe-eyed stare of a boy in way over his head.

"What can I do?" asked Torie.

He just blinked rapidly a few times, before pointing to a tablet that sat at the end of a long counter, blinking with waiting orders that Fionna was sending in. Torie took one look at the list and nodded.

"Okay. First, just breathe. Second, we got this," she said with a wink.

And forty-five minutes later, they were looking at the last order of biscuits, gravy, and pan-fried apples going out to a couple of patrons sitting in the far corner of the bakery and cafe, whispering quietly to one another.

In the silence following the morning rush, Fionna gathered everyone around the register to sing their praises.

"You guys! That was amazing. I can't believe we pulled that off. I mean...I can absolutely believe it. Because I have the greatest team, the greatest friends, and the greatest wife to ever walk the Earth!" She was beaming with pride as she reached for her two new recruits. "Tara, Nicholas, these are my best friends Torie and Jasmin, and, of course, you know Glen."

Glen smiled and waved. "Great work. And thank you, Torie and Jasmin for jumping in. You saved us back there."

"Somehow I think it's us who should be thanking you," Jasmin replied with a smile.

"It's really great to meet you," said Tara, speaking up. "Fionna has told us all about you."

Torie lifted an eyebrow in Fionna's direction. "Well, I

hope not everything. Some things are better left discovered than told."

Fionna rolled her eyes in an exaggerated manner while giving her friends a bright smile. "Don't go fretting. I left you some secrets."

Nicholas seemed a bit perplexed but offered a shy smile, nonetheless. He wore round, wire-framed glasses and pushed at them with his forefinger as he nodded in Torie's direction. "Thank you, ma'am, for helping out. You were a wiz in the kitchen. I don't think I'll ever be as good as you at handling all that."

Torie laughed and shook her head. "My name is Torie, not ma'am. And you did an amazing job. The trick in preparing a big meal—and breakfast rush is just one big meal—is to develop your own system and get it perfected. You'll have yours down in no time, I'm sure."

"Okay, if you have this under control, I need to get going," said Glen, removing her apron. "Contrary to what some may think, I do have a job of my own to attend." She smiled coyly at Fionna and gave her a quick kiss on the cheek before waving to everyone and heading out the door.

Tara and Nicholas headed into the kitchen to start cleaning up and preparing for the lunch push, while Fionna agreed to take care of the few stragglers that remained.

"So, how did it go last night?" Fionna asked. "Did you find the plants you were after?"

"And then some," said Jasmin. "You are not going to believe what we stumbled across. Well, actually, you probably will."

A beep from Torie's phone interrupted the conversation. She looked up after checking her screen. "That's going to have to wait. Emil just texted. He's already found something very unusual with the body."

She turned on her heels, heading for the door, with Jasmin close behind.

"Hey, wait," Fionna called after them. "What body? You can't just leave me hanging like this. And what about the lunch crowd?"

Jasmin threw her a smile over her shoulder. "Those kids are great! You got this, girl. See you soon."

And with that, they were out the door, into Torie's sleek BMW, and heading for the medical examiner's office.

Chapter Four

The office of Dr. Emil Faun was a single story, brick building located on the backside of the Singing Falls Community Hospital. It sat back from the main building, separated by an expansive parking lot, with a large, canopied overhang where emergency vehicles could pull up and easily transport bodies in and out without being seen by the visitors and patients of the main building.

Torie parked in front and headed for the large sliding glass doors with Jasmin at her side. Dr. Faun was waiting patiently just inside the main entry and smiled warmly, leading them through a narrow, dimly lit hallway towards his private office.

Inside, the office was as sterile and sparsely furnished as the rest of the building. Along one wall ran a series of metal cabinets, and an imposing desk of steel and glass squatted against another. Under the eerie green glow of the computer monitor sat three distinct blue folders, each perfectly aligned in a row. A single pen and notepad were the only other items sitting out in the open.

Emil led them through a set of doors at the back of his office into a second, smaller room. This one contained a deep, steel sink, with a large, stainless faucet. Next to it hung an array of medical gowns above a rack containing shoe covers, gloves, and surgical masks.

He stopped next to the rack of protective equipment and gestured to the two women. "You'll need to put on the shoe covers and a mask please." He grabbed a pair of shoe covers for himself and stepped into them before putting on a face mask. They could tell that the practiced ease with which he donned the gear came from years of practice, and they found themselves hurrying to keep pace with the doctor.

He gave them a quick visual check before pushing through the final set of metal doors into the exam room proper.

Torie looked around, taking the space in. It wasn't what she expected. In the movies, these rooms were always gray and dimly lit with the body of someone lying on a tiny, metal table, a single goose-necked lamp shining down on them. But this space was expansive and so bright it almost hurt her eyes.

A single stainless-steel table dominated the center of the room, sitting above a drain in the floor that reflected the adjustable lighting that hung from tracks crisscrossing the ceiling. Along the walls were computer monitors and cameras to document every step of an autopsy from start to finish. Various pieces of equipment were laid out on rolling tables sitting at precise intervals throughout the room, including scalpels, probes, saws, and clamps – all of which could be used to determine various causes of death. Looking around, Torie knew that Dr. Faun had access to some of the finest medical technology available.

They made their way to the table and were faced with the outline of a body covered by a black drape. Beside it, there was a trolley also covered by a drape made of the same material.

Emil reached for the cover over the body, but then stopped, looking at the witches. "You're not squeamish, by any chance, are you?"

"Unfortunately, this isn't our first dead body. I'm sure we've seen worse," said Jasmin.

Emil gave a little nod and carefully peeled back the cover to reveal the body of the man they had found. All his clothing had been removed and his body had been cleaned of residue. His skin was a taut, pale, lifeless gray. Torie had a feeling it would feel like wax paper stretched over cold hamburger if she touched it, which she had no intention of doing.

Their eyes were drawn to the Y-incision that started at each of the man's shoulders, came together at mid-chest, and then continued in a single line down his abdomen. Thankfully, it was stapled shut, keeping his innards concealed from view.

"Wow. You work fast, Emil," Torie said. "You did all this in the short time the body's been here?"

The examiner nodded. "Well, I utilize a combination of technology and...slightly more esoteric resources, to find what I am looking for. And in this case, I had a feeling time was of the essence. More so than usual."

"And what did you find?" asked Jasmin.

"Caucasian male, middle-aged—I'd say late forties—in decent, but not great, health and shape. Well off—"

Torie held up a hand. "How can you tell his economic standing?"

"There are no signs of disease or malnutrition, no

lasting trauma or injury that
care, his teeth are in excelle
always taken good care of hin
very expensive wristwatch that no
his wallet contained multiple credit
hundred dollars in cash."

"The money wasn't removed? And
taken? Doesn't sound like it was a robbery,"

"No. There is no trauma to the body that i
there was a struggle of any type either," said h
he's human. I removed all his internal organs—" he
to the trolley next to them, "—and his internal bone
ture is that of a normal human male. No signs of bein
shifter or any other type of supernatural."

"Do you know what killed him?" asked Torie.

The little sprite gave them a wry smile, nodding his head. "He was poisoned with a very rare substance called Shadow Venom. It was administered via the tips of a pine needle here." He pointed to a place just behind the man's ear. There was a pinpoint of discoloration so slight that Torie and Jasmin had to bend uncomfortably close to see it. "Shadow Venom is a highly toxic compound designed to find weaknesses in a victim's physiologic structure and amplify it to the point of death, thereby causing the death to appear natural. In this man's case, he was in the beginning stages of heart disease. The venom accentuated that, causing him to die by a heart attack."

Jasmin frowned. "I've never heard of Shadow Venom."

"Very few have," Emil responded. "It's a tricky substance to make and administer. It can just as easily kill the person creating it as it can the intended victim."

"Emil, how quickly does this poison act?" asked Jasmin.

"Within minutes of being administered," he answered.

t means that it wasn't given to him until after he
up the mountain. There's no way to access the
via vehicle, so unless someone carried him there
killing him, he was killed onsite," said Torie.

Now that I can confirm," said Emil. "Going by his
y temperature, he died a couple of hours before you
und him."

Torie frowned, staring at the doctor. "But how can that
be? I mean, he was completely covered over by vegetation
and growth."

Emil raised a finger. "About that...that's why I called you
here. That's the strange part."

"Wait, being killed by something called Shadow Venom
isn't strange enough?" asked Jasmin.

"This body was not supposed to be found," said Emil.
"It was probably just luck that you stumbled upon it when
you did. In another few hours it would have been gone
completely."

"How is that possible?" asked Torie.

"Well, at the site, I noticed something very peculiar. Not
about the body per se, but the dirt around it." Emil led
them around the table to a metal worktop bolted to the wall.
On it sat a couple of microscopes, a computer, and an array
of high intensity desk lights. "At first, I wasn't sure what I
was smelling around the body. It was something mixed in
with the dirt that didn't belong there. The fact that Max
couldn't smell anything was my first clue what we were
dealing with. Luckily, when I got a sample back here, I was
able to confirm my suspicions."

He reached for a small, marble bowl on the table and
showed the contents to the witches.

Jasmin shrugged. "Looks like dirt to me."

"To your eyes, yes. To mine, and to my nose, there was

something not right about it. Turns out, the area where this man was buried was coated in hardwood ash—most likely from a beech tree. That is why it didn't give off any out-of-the ordinary scent to Max," Emil said.

"Okay. And?" said Torie.

"And," he continued, "hardwood ash is the key ingredient in making lye. All that is needed to start the process is water. The best kind of water being rainfall."

Jasmin's eyes grew wide as realization crept in. "Growing up poor in the mountains, we used to make our own lye soap. That stuff could eat through anything in its pure form."

"Exactly," said Emil.

"But you also have to heat the mixture to make it truly caustic," said Jasmin. "You said had we not found it the body would have been completely dissolved in hours. Hardwood ash and water alone can't do that."

Emil nodded. "You're right. Under normal circumstances, it would not." He made his way to the large sink and returned with a paper cup containing water. "Stand back a little."

They did as he asked and watched as he placed the bowl of dirt away from everything else on the table and then proceeded to carefully pour the water into it.

The water barely made contact with the dirt before a swift and violent reaction occurred. The contents of the bowl began to smoke and bubble, turning black, then brown, then orangish-red. Even standing back, the two women could feel the heat it was giving off as the mixture churned and bubbled. Then, just as quickly as it began, it was over. Everything settled down and as they peered carefully into the bowl, only brown soil remained.

"What the heck was that?" Jasmin said.

Emil raised both eyebrows in dismay. "That was magic. Nature corrupted to something very dark. Namely, destroy a murder victim and leave no trace evidence."

"Without burning down the land around it, I assume," said Torie.

"Exactly. It would be contained to only the area of the conflagration. Everything else would remain untouched. Had it started raining before you arrived, no one would ever know a crime had been committed."

Jasmin's brow was knitted in a frown as she began to pace back and forth. "Emil, I've heard of this before, but I've never come across it in practice."

Torie studied her friend. "Jasmin, do you know who did this?"

Jasmin turned to face her, letting out a deep breath. "Not their identity, no. But there is only one force that could have created this. Hedge witches."

Now it was Torie who frowned. "We've encountered a hedge witch before, but she didn't demonstrate anywhere near this level of magic."

Jasmin shook her head. "We were up against an apprentice then, someone who had not mastered all that a hedge witch is capable of. This is something entirely different. This is the work of a master hedge witch. Someone capable of harnessing the power of a hedge coven."

Torie's mind was racing as she looked at them. "You know, the Fate Sisters told us there were other witches in the area. But wouldn't we have sensed it if they were malevolent?"

"Not necessarily," replied Jasmin. "Hedge witches can evade our senses because they aren't tied into the same magic that we are. Historically, hedges and hexes don't mix."

"How could we have missed this?" Torie wondered. "I mean, there's no way that an entire coven of hedge witches is operating in or around Singing Falls and we not know. Right?"

"Wrong," came a voice from behind them.

They turned just as Max was walking through the metal doors with Elric at his side.

The two werewolves walked up to them; their faces masks of worry.

"What do you mean wrong, Max?" Jasmin asked.

The wolves exchanged glances before Max spoke. "There is a coven of hedge witches operating in Crest Haven, the town just next door to Singing Falls."

Chapter Five

Jasmin took in a deep breath and fixed the wolf with a stare that would have stopped a semi in its tracks. "And you're just now telling us about this?"

Max winced as if he had been physically struck. "It never really seemed like a big deal. I mean, what's a few more witches in a community full of supernaturals?"

Torie took a deep, calming breath. "You know what happened the last time we crossed paths with a hedge witch. How long have you known?"

The sheriff looked confused. "I don't know. A year, I guess."

Power thrummed off Jasmin as she glared at the werewolf.

Max pointed feebly at Elric. "He knew too."

Elric gave his best friend an exasperated look, dropping his arms to slap against his sides. "Oh great...drag me into this."

"Wait. Elric, what are you doing here?" asked Torie.

Elric walked over to Torie and gave her a quick kiss. "Max called me about the body."

"I figured he could go with me to check out the dead man's place. We were able to pull his address from the name on the credit cards and his ID," said Max.

"Is he from here in town?" Torie asked.

Max shook his head sheepishly. "Actually, he's from Crest Haven."

Jasmin gave Torie a wide-eyed stare while pursing her lips. "Of course he is. Could this be a coincidence?"

"You know what I think about coincidences," replied Torie. "No such thing."

"So, doc, what did you find out?" Max asked.

The examiner quickly filled the two wolves in on his findings, ending with the revelation that this had to be the work of hedge witches. "And that's where you two walk in. So now everyone is on the same page."

"Max, do you know any of the police or detectives in Crest Haven?" Torie asked.

He thought for a second before nodding his head. "Maybe. There is one detective I've crossed paths with before. But I'm not sure how much help she'll be."

"Why's that?" Jasmin asked.

"Well, unlike Singing Falls, Crest Haven is pretty much a mundane town. There aren't really any supernaturals there. The only magical element is probably the hedge witches. And they tend to keep a very low profile."

"So, you know where to find them?" It was a question, but everyone in the room knew it was more of a statement.

"Why?" asked Elric, narrowing his eyes.

Jasmin stepped forward, pointing at the wolves. "Because the two of you are going to check out where our Mr.—" Her voice trailed off as she pointed at the body.

"Jeffries. Clive Jeffries," said Max.

"Where our Mr. Clive Jeffries lived, and see what his family may or may not know. And Torie and I are going to pay a friendly welcome-to-the-neighborhood visit to those hedge witches."

Max held up a finger. "Well, technically, they aren't new to the neighborhood. They've been here——" And again, Jasmin's look froze him in place.

"Or I could just text you the address of where they meet up, and you can go introduce yourselves."

Elric opened his mouth to speak but was instantly cut off by Torie.

"Yes, Elric?" she asked, making sure her tone conveyed there really wasn't an opening. "Did you want to add something?"

The wolf's mouth closed, and he shook his head.

"Good. Then you'll let us know what you find, and we'll let the two of you know what we find out. Sound like a good plan?"

"Hey, if you like it, I love it," said Max, ignoring the look Jasmin tossed his way. "Come on, Elric, let's get going."

Elric made his way over to Torie and pulled her close. "I know I don't have to say it...but be careful."

"Right back at you," she replied, stretching up on her tiptoes to give him a quick kiss. "Tell Max not to forget to send us that address."

He nodded and disappeared out the doors, following his friend.

"Well, looks like we get to pay a visit to a new coven," Torie said to Jasmin.

"Not just yet. It would be considered the height of rudeness to show up empty-handed. Let's swing by your place first. I have an idea for a gift we can whip up for them."

"And I'll do a deeper dive into more of the samples I took from the crime scene," said Emil. "See if I can dig up anything else on these hedge witches."

A half-hour later, Torie and Jasmin had walked back into Torie's house to an ecstatic Leo. The little dragon was flying in circles in excitement.

"Geez, it's only been a few hours. You'd think he hadn't seen you in months," Jasmin laughed.

"He's always like that, aren't you, good boy? Yes, you are." Torie held out a finger and conjured a ball of orange light and sent it careening through the house. Leo yelped happily and began chasing it. "That'll keep him busy for a bit. Now, what did you have in mind for a gift?"

"Follow me," said Jasmin. She led them down the stairs to the basement where there was a large, open space they had nicknamed The Sanctum. It was the most warded and protected space in the house, and it was where Torie practiced her magic.

The chamber was extraordinarily spacious, filled with inviting, comfortable furniture, tall bookcases adorned with strange symbols, flickering sconces in the shape of arcane characters, and a grand area rug of blue and green wool woven in hypnotic patterns. The atmosphere was warm and inviting, providing the perfect setting for a witch to practice spells that may or may not flare out of control at times.

In the center of the room was a large, ornate wooden table, with a couple of leather-bound books stacked to one end.

Jasmin made her way to the shelving units along one wall and retrieved a couple of glass bowls, which she handed to Torie, and a large, marble mortar and pestle, which she carried to the table. Torie placed the bowls next to the mortar and stood back, hands on hips.

"They could be killers, you know. And yet we're bringing them gifts?"

"And they might not be the killers," replied Jasmin. "If they are, we will deal with it. If they aren't, and we show up empty-handed, then it's a breach of etiquette that we will likely regret at some point in the future."

"Fine. But you still haven't told me what we're making. And what I can do to help."

Jasmin placed her hands flat on the table and leaned forward, smiling at Torie. "I've studied hedge magic, but never really ventured too far into the weeds with it, so to speak. But what I do know is that they stand firm on tradition rooted in nature. So, we are going to present them with a gift I don't think they will say no to. But first, we need the ingredients. Can you use your talent and bring us some clove, rosemary, sage, yarrow and of course some of my namesake, jasmine, from your greenhouse?"

Torie nodded and held out her hand. She used her calling magic, one of the first magical gifts she had discovered, to bring each of the plants to her. One by one, she called their name, and they appeared in her hand, having been transported through space in a swirl of orange dust from her greenhouse to reappear at the table before them. "Okay, now what?"

"Now, I show you how to create a Good Fortune Charm Potion. It is a charm that is meant to bless a witch with good luck and prosperity in nature. Made with these plants and roots and infused with just a touch of our own hex magic."

Torie watched as she gathered the plants and, one by one, added bits of them to the mortar. "And the significance of these particular plants?"

Jasmin spoke as she slowly began to crush the plants together. "Clove is for protection against negative energy. Rosemary is for luck and good fortune. Sage grants wisdom and guidance. Yarrow adds courage and strength, and Jasmine is for happiness and joy."

She finished grinding the ingredients, and then rubbed her hands together over the mortar, before pouring the powdered mixture into the glass bowl.

"Now all we need are a few drops of morning dew and then we bind it into a potion."

"I have the dew here," Torie said, moving to another shelf and retrieving a tiny brown bottle. She also gathered a delicate, crystal perfume bottle. "Will this work to collect the potion in?"

"It's perfect." Jasmin took the two bottles and sat them down. Then, opening the brown bottle, she carefully introduced two drops of a shimmering liquid into the bowl containing the mixture. Then she spoke in a whispered voice.

"I conjure a charm of protection and peace,
so it might bring the owner all that they seek."

The magic in her words wrapped around the mixture, drawing out the power of the plants and fusing it into a blue potion that sparkled in the glass bowl. Opening the perfume bottle, Jasmin breathed another bit of magic into the bowl and the potion swirled into the air before settling into the tiny crystal bottle. She placed the stopper, sealing the bottle, and held it up for Torie to inspect.

"And now we have a gift to present," she said.

"It's beautiful," Torie said. She checked her phone and nodded in Jasmin's direction. "Max sent the address. Let's go feed Leo and then head over there."

Together, they headed up the stairs and into the main hall that led to the kitchen. Torie held up her hand, summoning the orange ball of light she had left for Leo back to her hand. The little dragon followed behind, his wings vibrating in the air as he landed on the kitchen island. His emerald eyes watched Torie closely as she moved to the refrigerator.

"Leo, Mommy and Auntie Jazzy are going out to run an errand, but I will be right back. You be a good boy and watch the house." She bent over, rummaging through the lower drawer where she kept the dragon's steak. "Do you want your dinner? Is my baby ready for some food?"

"Yes, much food."

The reply was gruff and mangled, the words chopped and drawn out.

Torie froze, then slowly raised her head, looking at the dragon facing her. Then she looked to Jasmin, whose eyes were giant orbs as she stared first at Leo, then Torie, and back to Leo.

"Did...did you hear that?" asked Torie. "Was that in my head? Or did...?"

Jasmin was nodding slowly. "Your dragon just spoke."

Chapter Six

Both witches were awestruck, not quite sure what to do next.

"Do it again," said Jasmin in a fast whisper. "Make him speak again."

Torie never took her eyes off Leo but turned her body slightly in her friend's direction. "I didn't make him do anything. This is the first time something like this has happened." She slowly walked over to the dragon who was regarding her with an inquisitive stare. "Leo, little one...did you just say something to Mommy?"

The dragon cocked his head to one side, looking from Torie to the refrigerator and back again.

Torie followed his eyes before speaking again. "Yes, that's right. Does little Leo want some food? Ask for it. What do you want?"

Leo looked at her as if he was genuinely confused, large eyes blinking rapidly.

"Maybe he didn't say it aloud," Torie said. "I mean, we share a mental rapport, so he could have just projected his thoughts. Or something like that. I mean, he's a dragon...we really don't know what he's capable of."

Jasmin nodded. "Well, we may not know what he can do, but I definitely heard him speak. And I heard it with my ears. He said those words out loud."

Torie stood back, shaking her head. "Well, we can deal with a potentially talking dragon later. For now, we need to get over to Crest Haven." She returned to the fridge, casting one last look at her dragon before fishing out some raw meat and dumping it into a large dog dish. "Okay, have at it."

Leo took to the air, landed quickly at the dish, and buried his face in his meal, greedily gulping down whole chunks of meat at time.

"I don't even want to know what you're going to spend keeping him fed as he grows," Jasmin said.

"That makes two of us. I'll be back later, Leo."

And with that the two of them headed towards the front door. Torie turned to her friend. "Hey, can you text Emil? Have him send us a couple of photos of that body."

"Sure. What are you planning?"

"Just a hunch," Torie replied as they walked out the door and into the evening air. With a thought, she reinforced the wards around the house, and then climbed into Jasmin's SUV.

The town of Crest Haven was roughly an hour away and they passed time by discussing talking dragons, new spells that could be created from the harvested lunarwort, and of course, dead bodies found entombed in magical charged dirt that was designed to destroy it as soon as the rains came.

"And that's another point," said Torie. "Did you know it was going to rain? Cos I didn't. If I had known, I would have never suggested going up onto a mountain to pick flowers."

Jasmin shook her head as she followed the directions being given to her by the pleasant but robotic-sounding navigation system. "I did not. But that's a good point. If rain wasn't forecast, then maybe whoever did the killing didn't plan this out the way we are thinking."

"Unless they created the rain. Can hedge witches do that? You said their magic is based in nature, right? Could part of that magic include making it rain?"

Jasmin thought for a second before shrugging her shoulders. "I don't know. For all our power, I doubt you or I could make it rain. But, when it comes to magic, there are forces out there that we still know very little about."

They passed a sign that told them they were entering the city limits for Crest Haven, and soon the pleasant robot voice told them to take a right turn onto a two-lane stretch of road bordered with patches of grass and dirt to either side, and then nothing but towering trees beyond that.

"It's going to be dark by the time we arrive," said Torie.

"That's okay. They're witches, not vampires."

Torie ignored her friend's sarcasm and focused on the impenetrable bank of trees outside her window. Much quicker than either of them expected, the navigation announced that they had arrived at their destination.

Jasmin stopped the car and they both looked around.

"I don't see anything," she said.

Torie was about to respond when something ahead of them and to the right caught her eye. It was the top of a house, just peeking through the tree line. "There. I think that's a house."

Jasmin eased the car forward, and sure enough another quarter mile brought them to a grand, gated entry of black iron anchored by stone monoliths to either side. As the car drew closer, the gates swung inward, letting them pass.

The drive led to a circular pull through. At the apex of the circle sat a house. That is, if you could call it that. Torie had seen grand hotels that were smaller.

The house was gothic in nature, imposing in its grandeur. The mansion reared up from the earth like a living beast, its towering spires clawing at the oppressive night sky. Windows stared down at them, casting menacing shadows over the landscape. More chimney stacks than the witches could count lined up along the spine of the roof like sentinels, a silent warning to any who dared disturb the solitude of this majestic manor.

"And I thought we were rich," Jasmin said as they exited the car.

Torie closed her eyes, preparing to send out a wave of magic to probe the imposing structure, but Jasmin stopped her before she could cast the spell outward.

"No. Don't do that. It would be an affront to them."

Reluctantly, Torie let the spell die, feeling it dissipate into the ether around them. Taking a deep breath, the two of them walked up the many steps leading to the large front porch and the grand double doors carved from mahogany.

On each of the steps were ornate planter boxes filled with green, leafy plants that shimmered and vibrated at the witches passing. Torie stared at them, then at Jasmin, who only nodded in response.

"Hedge witch version of wards, I believe," Jasmin said.

Standing before the doors, they hesitated briefly and exchanged looks.

"Too late to turn back now," said Torie as she reached for a large, brass knocker in the shape of a ring protruding from the carved head of a stag's nose. When she rapped the ring against the door, the antlers of the stag began to glow, and she could feel a ripple of magic pass from the door knocker into the house.

They waited for a few seconds, and then the large doors were pulled open. Standing before them was a mountain of a man. He was older, perhaps in his late fifties, but the way his button-down white shirt and form-fitting gray trousers struggled to contain his muscular physique, the witches knew he had to be more than just human. At close to seven feet tall, he towered over them, looking down as if he spotted a couple of insects that needed to be squashed.

"Can I help you?" he asked, his voice booming in its resonance.

Even Jasmin seemed at a loss for words as she looked up into the man's stone-cold face. "We are...um...I mean, we are here...can you..."

Torie stepped forward, steeling her voice. "We're here to speak with whoever is in charge of this area's coven of hedge witches."

The giant fixed her with a stare before responding. "Wait here." He slammed the door in her face, leaving her to look questioningly at Jasmin.

Finally, the door opened again.

"This way," the giant said in his booming bass.

The witches followed him inside and were welcomed by a grand foyer. It was two stories tall with a large, circular chandelier of rough iron hanging from impressive steel chains.

They followed the giant through the entry and down a wide, marble hallway lined with black sconces in the shape of gargoyles.

"We get it, you're goth," Torie scoffed, whispering in Jasmin's ear. Jasmin admonished her with a slight elbow as they passed beyond a gracious, double staircase curving upwards to a dark landing. Torie strained her neck but could not see a ceiling in the towering structure.

They reached the end of the passageway and came to a set of closed, double doors. The giant stepped aside, sweeping one hand forward at the doors.

"Oh, okay," said Jasmin. "I guess we just go right in." She placed her hand on the latch, pushing it down and swinging the door inward.

The room beyond was as open and opulent as the rest of the house. It was built in a circle, with tall twenty-foot windows overlooking an expansive back yard. The part of the space that was not all glass functioned as a home library, with countless custom bookshelves lining the walls. There were steps on two different walls leading up to a second landing that was also all bookshelves, packed with tomes of all sizes.

The furniture below consisted of tables made from the same wood as the shelves with smooth leather reading chairs centered around them. They were situated in clusters to form areas for intimate discussion and quiet reading or just sitting in thought without interruption or distraction.

The lighting was dim, consisting of atmospheric lamps and gothic overhead chandeliers that gave off a warm, amber hue.

Despite herself, Torie was impressed at what spread out before them.

The two witches were so engrossed in the sheer

magnitude of the room that they almost didn't notice the people milling about. Inside there were easily a dozen or more adults scattered throughout the library. Some were holding open books, others were sitting together with coffee cups in hand, talking quietly among themselves. All of them stopped what they were doing and turned their heads in Torie and Jasmin's direction when the witches entered the room, and an eerie silence settled over the space.

Movement out of the corner of her eye caught Torie's attention and she turned to see a tall, striking figure dressed from head to toe in a form-fitting black, long sleeved shirt, and a matching skirt that came to just above black high-top boots. Her long silver hair was pulled back in a high ponytail that swayed slowly from side to side as she approached.

Up close, Torie could see the woman was of indiscernible age, but most likely in her early fifties. She wore silver earrings that dangled from her lobes, and a single silver choker around her neck that clasped in front. Black, rectangular glasses framed her purple eyes.

"Well, well, well," said the woman, her voice silky and smooth. "And to what do we owe this pleasure?"

Jasmin squinted at the woman as she approached. "I'm sorry, what?"

The woman stepped to within three feet of them and smiled. "The famous Jasmin and Torie. Hex witches deciding to bless us with their presence for some reason. I'm just asking what that reason is."

Without looking around, Torie could feel all eyes on them as she stretched out an arm, extending her hand to the woman who was obviously in charge. "Hi, you already seem to know our names, but I'm Torie, and this is Jasmin." She took the woman's hand and shook. "And since we seem to be at a slight disadvantage, I'd love to know who I have the pleasure of speaking with."

The woman stared at their two hands as Torie moved them up and down. It was almost as if it were a custom she was entirely unfamiliar with. Then, she smiled, and politely withdrew her hand.

"I am Eliza. I lead this coven."

As one, the adults in the room made their way towards the three women, gathering at Eliza's back. As one, they reached in their jackets and vests and drew a gnarled wooden stick with bits of evergreen leaves growing from the ends of them. With a whisper the leaves began to glow and were all pointed at Torie and Jasmin.

Eliza smiled again. "Now give me a reason not to have my witches blast the two of you to kingdom come."

Chapter Seven

The crackle of magic filtering through the air was palpable. Torie felt Jasmin's hand on her back, helping to ease the tension that suddenly filled her body.

"Well, if you did that, how would we present you with this welcome gift?" said Jasmin. "We are just here to intro-duce ourselves, meet our neighbor witches, and welcome you to the community." She reached into her purse, and the action elicited a murmur of voices from everyone around them. Slowing her motions, she carefully lifted the potion into the air for all to see. "It's something we created just for this coven."

She looked at Eliza, holding the bottle in her outstretched hand. The leader of the coven nodded to her, and Jasmin slowly approached, handing her the potion.

"It is a charm. A Good Fortune Potion," said Jasmin. "Formulated specifically for you."

Eliza took the potion and closed her eyes, wrapping her hand around the delicate crystal bottle. When she opened her eyes, there were motes of gold floating around the purple of her irises.

"Does it look like we need help from you to achieve fortune?" came a voice from just behind the coven leader.

A young woman stepped from between two of the older adults and made her way forward. She had bright, inquisitive eyes, a slim form and silver hair pulled back in a ponytail that mimicked her leader's. She focused her defiant eyes on Torie and Jasmin.

"Ah, Torie, Jasmin, this is Malena," said the coven leader. "My daughter."

Standing next to her mother, Torie and Jasmin could see the striking physical similarity between the two women. But that was where the comparison ended. Where the mother stood calm and assured, and her eyes met those of the newcomers with a kind of quiet strength and intelligence, here the daughter was all tension and nervous darting glances. Her purple eyes swept to and fro, not locking onto the gazes of the witches as her mother's had.

"It's nice to meet you, Malena," said Torie. "And you are right; you don't seem to need any blessings from anyone."

The young woman, looked briefly at her mother and then down at her feet.

"But this is not just any old charm," said Jasmin. "It is imbued with our own magics. A gift just for you."

One of Eliza's eyebrows shot up dramatically. "And to think I've always been told to be wary of hexes bearing gifts. In any case, that changes nothing." She handed the potion to her daughter as she rolled her eyes. "Put this some place safe."

Torie frowned, biting her tongue to keep from saying something she might later regret. She watched as Malena left her mother's side, taking the charm potion with her. "A thank you is the usual response to a gift."

They felt the room bristle with magic at Torie's words, and Jasmin quickly stepped forward trying to de-escalate the situation.

"Please forgive our intrusion," she said, glancing at Torie. "If we caught you at a bad time, we apologize. But we only just found out about your coven. There are so few witches in the community, we just couldn't wait to drop by and say hello."

"And is that all you wanted to say?" said Eliza. "Or did you come by to maybe see what we were up to? Maybe to tell us that our kind isn't welcome here. That our magic is not quite good enough for you hexes."

Again, a murmur of voices rose, and magic prickled in the direction of Torie and Jasmin. Only this time, Torie took offense at both the woman's words and the actions of her coven.

"No, that's not true at all. We are welcoming of everyone, no matter what type of magic they might practice," Torie said.

"Oh, we've heard of how welcoming Singing Falls can be to other magic practitioners," said Eliza.

"What's that supposed to mean?" Torie asked, narrowing her eyes. "We treat everyone just as they would treat us."

"Then be open with us," said Eliza. "What is it you really want?"

"Fine," said Torie, stepping forward. "By any chance, were you or any members of your coven practicing rituals up on Cone Bluff Mountain at any time late last night?"

Eliza stared at the witch before answering with a single word. "Why?"

And that was when both Torie and Jasmin felt it. The tiniest flicker of magic as the coven leader drew on just enough magic to gather some mental shields about herself. Reflexively, Torie reached out, her own magic grazing at Eliza.

The woman jumped, as if she had been physically struck.

"How dare you raise your magic to me," she said, indignation flaring in her voice.

"No, I didn't...I mean, I didn't mean to do it. I felt—" Torie started.

"What you felt was the need to assert your dominance over us," shot back Eliza.

Torie was shaking her head. She meant to apologize, but before she could, she felt a stinging lance of magic prick at the back of her neck. It was as if someone had pricked her skin slightly with a needle. It didn't hurt, but it startled the witch, and she spun, two magical fireballs racking into existence around her outstretched hands.

The coven hissed, drawing back from her and pointing their wands in her direction.

"Torie! What are you doing?" hissed Jasmin.

"Didn't you feel that?" she said, her brow knitted with confusion. "I mean...I felt...something."

"What you should feel is embarrassment," said Eliza, stepping forward. "You come here under the guise of peace, and then you threaten us with—" she glanced at Torie's glowing hands, "—your fire magic?"

Torie recalled her power, slowly raising her hands above her head. "I am sorry, Eliza. I don't know what happened there."

"What happened is these hex witches have come looking to put us in our places. It's just like Eliza said!"

It was a shout from one of the coven members, a woman, standing closest to Torie and Jasmin.

There was a rush of agreement, then another—this time a young man—spoke up, loudly. "They think no one is good enough to practice magic but them. They want to strip us of our powers."

The energy in the room was ramping up, like raw electricity looking for an iron rod to take to ground.

"None of that is true," said Jasmin. "We came here only to make introduction, and yes, there was a disturbance at Cone Bluff last night, but if you say you had nothing to do with it—"

Torie stepped towards Eliza, reaching into her pocket. She ignored the wands that sprang in her direction and instead took out her phone and pulled up the picture that Emil had texted her. "Do you recognize this man?" She thrust the phone at Eliza's face.

The coven leader looked at the screen and replied without a blink. "I do not. And I resent what you are implying here." This time, her purple eyes sparked dangerously with silver as they focused on Torie and Jasmin. "If I had welcomed you here in the first place, I would say you've overstayed it."

She cast a glance toward the door. Torie and Jasmin followed her eyes and saw the giant now standing inside the room, his face set and determined as he locked the witches in a steely gaze.

"No need for that," said Jasmin. "We'll be going."

The coven members parted and lowered their wands as they passed through. The witches kept their heads held high as they walked towards the door.

Torie stopped and turned briefly towards the coven leader. "I really am sorry this took the turn it did. I look forward to seeing you again and working on building a true friendship."

She didn't wait for a reply but turned on her heels and followed Jasmin out of the library. In silence they walked back to the main entrance of the house where the giant stood by the open door silently.

"Uh, thanks," said Jasmin as they stepped out into the night air.

The only reply was the shutting of the large doors and the unmistakable sound of a heavy-duty lock falling into place.

"Well, that went over well," said Jasmin, leveling a look at her friend.

Torie sighed as they headed down the steps. "Honestly, I know it looks like it was, but that was not my fault." They continued heading for the car in silence. "Didn't you feel that back there? Something struck me."

Jasmin turned to her friend. "Of course I did. And while you were threatening to flambé everyone, I was trying to get a lock on where it came from."

Torie's eyes widened. "And did you?"

Jasmin sighed as she shook her head. "No. It was so quick and random. One minute it was there, the next...nothing."

"That was my fault," came a small voice from behind the car.

Both of the witches jumped, startled by the sudden appearance of Malena. The girl walked out from the back of the SUV to face the women.

"Where did you come from? Were you always standing there?" asked Jasmin.

Malena nodded. "I was trying a masking spell. Using

the wind and the gravel to blend in with everything. But I'm not very good at it. I couldn't hold it for too long."

Torie walked around the front of the car to stand next to Jasmin. "Malena, are you supposed to be out here?"

The girl shrugged. "Out here is one thing; talking to the two of you is another." She looked around quickly, her eyes almost shifty as they moved from the shadows of the tree to the giant house and everywhere in between.

She was afraid of something. Her behavior was far from the borderline aggressive stance she had assumed upon their first meeting.

"How can we help you, Malena?" Jasmin asked. "I don't think you'd be out here risking your mother's ire just to tell us goodnight."

Malena cast her worried eyes to her shoes as she kicked at a couple of pebbles. "No. She would not be happy at all."

"Why did you prick me with your magic?" Torie asked.

She looked up, her expression one of pleading as she wrapped one arm across her body to hug the other. "I didn't mean to do that. I was trying to just...tap you on the shoulder. To get your attention. But I'm not very good at magic. It doesn't work with me for some reason."

Torie smiled, feeling herself soften at the girl's words. "I'm sorry to hear that. But don't give up. I didn't even know there was such a thing as magic until I hit forty."

The girl's eyes widened. "Really?"

Jasmin chuckled softly. "Really. And between us, she's still not very good at it."

"Hey," said Torie, giving her friend a playful poke.

Malena scrunched her face up, looking away from them again. "But the difference is you're hex witches. You tap into magic that hedges don't have access to. We can only do what we learn and are taught. And try as she might, my mother can't get me past the disconnect I have with nature. It just doesn't respond the way it should to me."

"You know, we would be happy to work with you," said Torie. "With your mother's permission, of course."

Malena frowned. "Yeah, that will never happen."

Torie and Jasmin exchanged glances. Jasmin cleared her throat to get the young woman's attention. "Malena, did you come out here to complain about your magic, or was there something else?"

Malena let out a nervous breath and started to rub her hands together as she studied the witches. "I think the coven is in danger, and my mom doesn't know how to protect them." She looked around, then leaned in to whisper. "Something is hunting us."

The fear on her face shook the witches to their core. An idea flashed through Torie's mind, and she took out her phone.

"Malena, we really want to help you. And we will. I hate to ask this of you, but do you recognize this man?" She pulled up the photo of the man who had been killed, and zoomed in so only his face filled the screen, not the beginnings of the Y incision or the metal slab of a table he was lying on.

The young woman took a look and gasped, stepping back with one hand covering her mouth.

"Malena," said Jasmin. "Do you know who this is?"

The girl nodded, eyes wide in fear. "That's my father."

Chapter Eight

Torie and Jasmin exchanged shocked looks as Torie placed her phone back in her jacket pocket. Malena's lip trembled as she bit back tears.

"Malena, I am so sorry for your loss," said Jasmin. "But I think this is something we need to speak with your mother about. When was the last time you saw your father?"

The girl's brow furrowed. "It's been a couple of years. We moved here from Portland to get away from him. My mother always said he was a bad man. She said he was after me."

"What can you tell us about—" Torie started.

A shout from the direction of the house caught their attention. Whirling around, Torie saw the male coven member who had spoken out against them in the library standing on the porch next to the giant and looking their way as he pointed. The giant began making his way down the stairs, eyes locked in their direction.

"Malena, we need—" Torie began, turning back to the girl. Only to find she was gone. A quick look around confirmed she was nowhere to be seen, so Torie hurried to the passenger side of the car and climbed in. "For someone who isn't very good at magic, she seems to have disappearing down pat."

"Buckle up, we need to go. Now," said Jasmin as she fired up the engine and pulled out of the drive.

Torie turned her head and saw more members of the coven rushing outside, glowing wands at the ready. As Jasmin accelerated, the coven grew smaller, until they disappeared completely from view.

"Do you think they knew we were talking to Malena?" said Torie.

Jasmin shook her head. "No way of knowing. But I do think that young woman can take care of herself. We need to concentrate on what our next steps are."

Torie sank back into the seats, deep in thought. "We need to speak with Eliza."

Jasmin looked over at her friend. "Yeah, like she is going to be so forthcoming with information. She practically just kicked us out of her house. We are most definitely persona-non-grata there."

"But that's just it. Why was she so aggressive with us? It was almost like she wanted to pick a fight. Something just felt off. And what if Malena was right and something really is hunting them? What if that something killed her father? Isn't it on us to help?"

Jasmin gripped the steering wheel tighter, her lips pursed. Finally, when she spoke, her words came out guarded. "Maybe this is not something we should get involved in. This is hedge witch business. Eliza is the leader of the coven and therefore it is her responsibility to keep them safe. I mean, we don't know the first thing about these people. Is that house Eliza's or is it communal? They obviously have some rudimentary control over magic, but what do they actually use it for? Why are they here? For that matter, what brought Eliza here from Portland? Was she running from something more than Malena's father? Did the coven follow her here or did she create this one once she arrived?"

Torie turned in her seat to face her friend. "Exactly. Those are all excellent questions and I think we need to find the answers to them."

"That isn't what I was getting at."

Torie smiled. "Weren't you though?"

Jasmin's face relaxed and she moved a finger up to tap her lips several times. "You know, they might have no reason whatsoever to speak with us. But they can't refuse to speak to an officer of the law investigating a crime." She turned and glanced at Torie.

Torie's eyes sparkled. "You're right. Except that Max doesn't have jurisdiction here, and there's no guarantee he can get cooperation from the locals here in Crest Haven."

"Maybe not. But I'm willing to bet Eliza is going to want to keep this quiet. Max could offer to speak to them under the guise that this stays on a need-to-know basis for the investigation."

"Meaning you and me as need-to-know," Torie finished. "That might work."

"Send him a text. Tell him to meet us back at your place to let us know what he and Elric found out."

Just then, Torie's phone pinged. She swiped the screen and laughed. "Speak of the devil. Elric is texting. Wants to make sure we are okay." She looked up at Jasmin before responding. "That's odd."

"Why would that be odd? Your overprotective, werewolf boyfriend is always worried about you."

"Yeah, but when he knows what we are doing, he's usually okay with it. Either they found something in the dead man's place, or he and/or Max knows more about these hedge witches than they are letting on." Her fingers raced over the screen as she typed a message back. "I told him we are on our way home and to bring Max to meet us."

"Sounds good," Jasmin said, returning her attention to the road.

"I just wish we could have spent a little more time talking to Malena. Or we could have found out more about what is going on inside that coven."

"Well, I think I can help us with that." She glanced over at Torie and gave her a mischievous smile. "I might have snuck a little something-something extra in that charm potion."

They arrived back at Torie's house moments before Max and Elric pulled up in Max's gray and white SUV with the words SF POLICE stenciled along the side. Torie disabled her wards to let Jasmin in, and then waited on the porch for the two wolves to enter.

"You okay?" asked Elric, throwing an arm around her waist as they walked through the door.

Torie eyed him suspiciously. "I'm fine. Just like I said in my text. Are *you* okay?"

Elric gave her the slightest of frowns but nodded.

"I take it you found something?" she said.

Before he could answer, Max called out from the kitchen. "Hey, do you have anything to eat in here?"

Torie rolled her eyes as she walked into the kitchen to see Max bent over, rummaging through the refrigerator.

"Gotta love those werewolf appetites," Jasmin said. "Especially around a full moon."

Torie looked questioningly at Elric.

"I mean, I could eat," he said sheepishly, running his hand through the back of his hair a couple of times.

Torie laughed and went to the pantry. "I'm sure I can whip up something for you two big, hungry wolves." She started rifling through cans of soup, boxes of crackers, bags of chips, and packages of ready-made snacks.

Max was back at the refrigerator, pulling out bottles of beer and stacks of cheese. He grabbed a plate from the cupboard and started snacking while pushing the cheese plate in Elric's direction. Elric plopped down at the island next to his friend and began picking at the pieces as well.

Torie made her way out of the pantry, arms full of goodies, including a large loaf of French bread. She looked at the plate of cheese the wolves were devouring and with a flick of her finger sent it sliding away from them. "How about grilled cheese and bacon sandwiches with tomato?" She glanced at Jasmin. "What about you? Fancy a little snack?"

The witch raised both shoulders. "Well, it would be rude to say no."

Torie smiled and made her way to the large range and fired up the middle grill section. The doors to one of the large built-in cabinets swung open and an array of cutlery and cooking utensils floated out to land on the island next to her.

"I will never get used to that," muttered Elric.

Jasmin laughed. "Well, you better. Considering you're going to be living here. We have come up with quite a few upgrades to the spell that powers this house."

"Great. I can't wait," the wolf replied.

"While Torie is throwing that together, care to tell us what you found at the dead man's place?" Jasmin asked.

"Clive. His name was Clive," answered Max. "And his place was clean. Too clean. Like it had practically been sterilized. Although we did find a suitcase in the bedroom closet. Something tells me he hasn't been in town long. We couldn't find anything concrete to connect him to the hedge witches though."

"Oh, we got that part covered," said Jasmin with a twinkle in her eyes.

Elric narrowed his in response. "What did you find?"

Jasmin began to recount the details of their meeting with the hedge witches, with Torie occasionally interjecting comments as she finished grilling bacon and was buttering thick pieces of French bread.

Jasmin's recitation ended with their encounter with Malena and her shocking revelation. "So, it seems like there is a connection between the coven and our victim."

"And we need you, Max, to take this to the next level," said Torie as she flipped the last sandwich over.

The house smelled amazing as the scent of melted butter, toasted bread, bacon and cheese filled the air. As expected, it wasn't long before Leo showed up, buzzing through the air to land at Torie's feet. His large, emerald eyes looking up in silent pleading.

Torie bent over and cooed at the little dragon. "Does baby want some food? Tell me. Tell Mommy what you want? Speak to me."

Elric and Max exchanged questioning glances.

"Um, is your lady okay?" asked Max.

"Of course she is," said Jasmin. "Leo spoke to us earlier and she's been trying to get him to do it again."

"Wait...the dragon spoke? Like, actual words? Out loud?" quizzed Elric.

Jasmin nodded. "Yep. Clear as a bell. Well, they were a little on the growly side, but they were definitely words."

Max puffed his cheeks out and picked up his beer. "The things you learn. But anyway, back to the hedge witches. What is it you want me to do?"

"Well," said Torie as she moved the sandwiches to plates for each of her friends, "Since this is now a murder investigation, we thought you could go and speak with the hedge witches. Make them answer some questions about the body that was found. If you go in an unofficial—but still official —capacity, they would have to speak with you."

Max frowned and Torie could tell he didn't like any of what she said. "What do you mean 'unofficial but official'? Crest Haven is not my jurisdiction."

"And we know that," she continued. "But you can tell them you know who and what they are, and that you have evidence linking hedge witches to the death. Tell them they can either talk to you—which keeps the conversation off the books—or you can open an official investigation with the local department in Crest Haven. My guess is they would rather keep this quiet. Especially if Crest Haven isn't known for dealing with supernaturals."

Max stopped mid-beer-swig. "That is a terrible idea."

"What? Why?" asked Jasmin.

"Because it will probably get him killed. Or worse," said Elric.

"Exactly," echoed Max. "And by 'or worse' he means getting me turned into a mouse or conscripted to the ground."

"They don't have the power to turn you into another living form," said Jasmin, scoffing at the idea.

Torie narrowed her eyes at the wolf. "And what does that mean? Conscripted to the ground?" Neither of the wolves spoke up, so Torie cleared her throat loudly, giving each a steely gaze as she fed slices of bacon to Leo.

Elric sighed as he turned to Jasmin. "Individually they may not have the power, but collectively, as a coven, it is most definitely something they are capable of. And more."

Max was nodding. "You've already seen an example of conscripting. It's when they command the earth to swallow someone alive and drain the energy from them. From what I hear, it's a terrible way to die. One they reserve for their most hated of enemies."

Now, both Torie and Jasmin stared hard at the wolves. Leo took one look at the witches and slowly slinked away, backing out of the kitchen with a mouthful of bacon.

"Do you mean to tell me that when you saw the crime scene you knew what it was? That this was the work of hedge witches?" demanded Jasmin.

Max bit the inside of his cheek, and Torie could see him measuring his words carefully.

"Not exactly," the wolf said. "I mean, I just thought someone was thrown into a shallow grave at first. But the more the doc kept poking around and mumbling to himself...and I heard him mention hardwood ash...well, it started to slowly come together."

"And you didn't think to mention it at the time?" Torie asked.

"I'm still a police officer, Torie. There was nothing to link the victim to the hedge witches, no conclusive proof that they were involved."

"At least not until Emil confirmed it and we provided the connection," said Jasmin.

Max nodded. "I should have said something, but hedge witches and werewolves don't exactly get along."

Something in his tone caught Torie's attention. "Is that why you knew they were operating one town over? You were keeping an eye on them because...you're scared of them? No. Not scared. You've had dealings with them before?"

Max held up both hands in a surrendering motion. "Not these particular ones. But yes. When we were running with our packs up North, we did have an encounter with a hedge coven. It wasn't pretty."

"What did they do?" asked Jasmin.

Max hesitated, staring at his hands. Finally, he spoke up. "They figured out a way to gain a new power. An aspect of the wolf."

His hands trembled as he paced the floor. Torie had never seen the wolf act like this, and though she dreaded the answer, she asked the question anyway. "How did they do that?"

He sighed and looked the witch in the eyes. "By skinning us, and then combining our pelts with their root magic and wearing them."

Torie gasped, covering her mouth with one hand.

Max placed his beer on the island with a heavy thud. "So, forgive me if I don't want to rush into a house full of supernaturals that can rip me out of my skin and wear it around like a fur coat."

Jasmin moved next to the big sheriff and placed a hand on his shoulder. "That will never ever happen, Max." Her eyes blazed bright green. "I promise you that."

"That's for sure," said Torie, her voice firm and low. "We'll find another way inside."

Jasmin looked up. "Tomorrow we will reach out to

Malena. I've a feeling she kept that charm vial we gave them close to her. I put a mirror spell on the bottle. It will allow us to communicate with anyone who stares into it."

Torie smiled. "Perfect."

"You have to be very careful when dealing with them," said Elric. His voice was filled with worry as he turned to Torie. "You've seen what one hedge witch can do, but you've never faced a coven."

"And they've never faced a hex witch," said Torie.

"Max, how did you defeat the hedge witches that were...doing what they did to your pack?"

The wolf took in a deep breath and let it out slowly. "When it comes to covens, they exist for one purpose. To take power from others and funnel it into their leader. That person is always the strongest among them. They protect and teach the rest of the coven. So, at great cost to our pack, we were able to separate their leader and kill her. When that happened, the coven dispersed and left our territory."

"And so now you think this hedge coven might be up to no good in this area?" Jasmin asked.

Max shrugged. "I don't know. All I know is that hedge witches ultimately only want one thing. Power. And considering Singing Falls is filled with an abundance of supernaturals..."

Torie shuddered. "Well, then all the more reason to find out what they are doing here, and what happened to Malena's father. Even if it means making another trip into the lion's den. And this time, maybe we won't be so nice."

Chapter Nine

Fionna smiled broadly as she opened the doors and stepped inside Brew Cup Bakery and Cafe. The couple of hours in the early morning before opening had become her favorite, when the predawn sky, still a deep navy blue, provided the perfect back drop for the quiet of the morning. In the twilight, there was a stillness to the world that slipped into everything. It felt like time slowed down, and it allowed her to enjoy all the little things that sometimes rushed by too fast for her to celebrate.

And here, morning hours in the bakery that she owned, had become her most favorite place and most favorite time —well second to time spent with Glen, of course.

But while Jasmin and Torie had been the investors in purchasing the bakery, Fionna had made it her own. From the contracts with local farmers and suppliers to utilize locally sourced ingredients, to the unique menu items only available in the bakery, to the new name that graced the front of the building. It was all Fionna, and she could not be happier.

She checked her watch, knowing there was a lot to be done before her employees showed up and the morning rush began. She had organized all her opening duties into a checklist and set about making sure everything would be ready.

She made sure all the equipment was in working order, checked her inventory as well as the expiration dates on ingredients, and then began to preheat the ovens. Next, she made her way into the main seating area and wiped down the already spotless tables and leather chairs arranged around the space. After that, she made her way to the display counter, cleaning the glass until it gleamed.

Working her way around the counter, she made sure the register was online and that there was enough cash in the drawer to start the morning, and then went back into the kitchen to check the tablet mounted on the wall. It received the online orders, and she wanted to make sure it was logged in , so they didn't miss any morning pickups from their more tech-savvy clientele.

The tinkling bell of the front door being opened caught her attention and she frowned, glancing at her watch. It was still too early for either of her staff. Plus, she was certain she had locked the bakery door behind her after coming in.

Wiping her hands, she made her way out of the kitchen to find someone standing at the register.

"Oh, I'm sorry, but we aren't open yet," Fionna said with a smile. "But if you'd like to leave an order with me, I'll be happy to make sure it's ready first thing when the doors open at seven."

The figure didn't move, but instead stared at the woman. "I need you to give a message to your friends for me."

Fionna frowned? "My...friends? Okay...well, let me get a pad and pencil."

"That won't be necessary. You are the message."

Before Fionna could say anything, the person before her raised her clenched fist and opened it palm up. She blew lightly into her hand, sending a silver cloud into Fionna's face.

The squirrel shifter gasped, sucking in a lungful of the powder, and felt her body seize up in response. The substance clogged her airways and burned her eyes.

The figure watched as Fionna fell backwards onto the floor, before turning and calmly walking out the door.

"I think we need more coffee before we try this," Torie said. "Or maybe we should wait until later in the day."

"It's almost dawn. I'm hoping Malena is up. And if she is, maybe she's near the charm potion and will respond to our summons," Jasmin replied.

"What makes you think she's up?"

"Because she wants to be a more powerful hedge witch. And dawn and dusk are times when all things in nature are stirring or settling down. It's when hedge witches are supposedly most attuned to their surroundings. It stands to reason that she will be up practicing magic. But we will see."

"Tell me again about this spell you snuck into the charm," Torie said. They were sitting in her office on either side of the large desk that took up one side of the room.

Rather than go to bed, they had opted to stay awake once Max had left and Elric had retired to the upstairs primary suite. Torie assured him she would be upstairs soon but had lost track of time as she and Jasmin plotted various ways to get back into the mansion where the hedge coven resided.

She yawned, stretching her hands over head, and almost as if on cue, the house responded to her need and two cups of steaming black coffee came floating into the study to settle on the desktop.

"Thank you," said Jasmin, reaching for the cup. "The spell we cast on this house seems to be growing and changing daily."

Torie frowned as she sipped the dark brew. "I can't tell if you think that's a good thing or a bad thing."

Jasmin arched an eyebrow. "That's because I haven't decided."

Torie laughed and watched as Jasmin placed a bowl of water they had brought with them into the study on the desk between them.

"Anyway," Jasmin said, "I placed a spell on the crystal bottle that turned it into a scrying crystal. Now, using water that has been enchanted with a matching incarnation, we can link the two. If someone else is around the bottle, we can reach out to them in a way that can't be detected by anyone else that is not in close proximity." She held her hand over the water and closed her eyes before chanting.

"I call on thee, oh objects of mine,
to open a channel that will intertwine."

The water in the bowl shimmered as a ripple passed through it. Then, with a slight glow, the transparency faded away and in its place a picture began to take shape. It was that of a large room, opulently furnished, with a large fireplace and four-poster bed dominating the space.

Then, muffled sounds began to float upward through the water, bubbling to the surface. At first, they couldn't make out the sounds they heard, but then, they realized it was someone crying. They continued to peer into the bowl until they saw a figure walking across the space, their back to the bottle.

They recognized Malena's silver hair as she moved slowly towards the door.

"Malena," Jasmin whispered softly into the bowl.

The young woman stopped in her tracks, her body stiffening. Slowly, she turned, searching for the source of the voice. Her face was puffy and her eyes red and swollen as she pressed a tissue to her nose. Tears were still flowing as she stared directly at the witches, shock and confusion slowly spreading across her features.

"Malena, don't be alarmed, it's us; Jasmin and Torie. Look at the charm bottle we gave you," Jasmin said.

Malena did as she was asked, stepping closer, her teary eyes widening.

"What's wrong?" asked Torie. "Did something happen to you?"

The woman's face changed from one of hurt and sadness to one of anger.

"How dare you!" she cried.

A hand reached for the bottle and then the image blurred as Torie and Jasmin felt themselves being hurled across the room. There was a sound of breaking glass, and then darkness as the water in the bowl became still.

Torie looked up in shock. "What just happened?"

Jasmin shook her head in dismay. "I have no idea. I mean, she should have been able to tell it was us."

"Can you try to reach out again and—" Torie was interrupted by her phone ringing. "Hold on a second, it's Fionna calling from the bakery." She placed the phone to her ear and her face froze before looking at Jasmin, eyes wide. "Okay, slow down...when did this happen?"

Jasmin came around the side of the desk, trying to listen in on the conversation.

"No, you absolutely did the right thing. We are on our way. Don't do anything until we get there," Torie said. She took the phone away from her ear and turned frantically to face Jasmin. "Something happened to Fionna. That was Tara, at the bakery. She is freaking out. Said they came in and found Fionna unresponsive." She looked past her friend, swallowing hard. "They think she's dead."

Chapter Ten

Jasmin was already following her friend out of the study. "Did they call 911?"

Torie was shaking her head. "She said Fionna had instructed her and Nicholas that if they ever ran into something that didn't seem right, especially if it involved her, they were to call you or me immediately. No questions asked." She grabbed her keys and headed for the door.

Jasmin had her phone in her hand as they hurried out. "I'm calling Emil to meet us there, just in case. Should we wake Elric?"

Torie was already climbing into the driver's seat. "Text him as well. Tell him to grab Max and get there as soon as possible."

The drive from her house to town was the fastest Torie had ever made in her life. She had no idea what was going on, but something in the young woman's voice told her everything was most definitely not alright with Fionna.

Jasmin had one hand planted firmly against the dashboard of the car, her phone cradled in the other as Torie gunned the engine. Normally, she would have been screeching at Torie to slow down, but she knew that time was of the essence in getting there. She had just finished leaving a message for Elric as they pulled into a spot in front of the bakery. Emil had picked up on the first ring and was already on his way to meet the women at the store.

They rushed in and both witches gasped at the sight that greeted them.

There, on the floor next to the counter, lay Fionna. Her body was in a state of rigor, hands open like claws, arms reaching upward, face contorted in a look of surprise with wide, unseeing eyes, and a mouth open in what appeared to be mid-scream.

"Bright Lady, have mercy," said Jasmin, dropping to her knees beside her friend.

"What in the world happened?" asked Torie. "You found her like this?" She turned to face Nicholas and Tara. The two frightened employees nodded in union.

"We came in through the back entrance as usual, hung up our coats, walked in and there she was," said Nicholas, his eyes not leaving Fionna's body.

"I have CPR training and I thought maybe she'd had a heart attack or something. Her pulse is weak, but I have meds to help that. She just doesn't seem to be responding," said Tara. "I didn't know what to do. I was going to call an ambulance, but then we remembered what she made us swear. To always call you two first."

Nicholas was shaking his head. "That's weird, right? We should have called 911. Or Glen. I mean, Glen's a nurse or paramedic or something, right? Shouldn't we have done that?"

The rising crescendo of his voice told Torie the young man was close to a full-blown panic. She saw Jasmin extend her arms over Fionna and immediately turned to face Tara and Nicholas, drawing their attention to her.

"Look at me," she said to the two of them. "You did exactly the right thing. We will let Glen know what is going on, but first I need you to tell me if you saw anyone else here when you arrived. Did you hear anything strange? Even if it was something you dismissed as your imagination."

"What?" asked Tara, confusion spreading across her features. "No. There was no one here when we arrived."

Nicholas nodded in agreement.

Torie looked around. "Was the front door locked when you got here? Because we were able to walk right in."

Nicholas thought for a brief second. "I don't know. We don't unlock it until we are ready to open the doors." A look of panic spread across his face again. "It's almost time to open. What do we do? Customers will be arriving soon."

Torie thought for a moment. "We can't open. We will put out a sign that says the equipment is down, or something like that. But we can't open. At least not yet. Tara, go and make that sign. Nicholas, if there are any standing or online orders, cancel them with a full refund and message the customer that their next order will be free." The two youngsters stared at her. "Now!"

They nodded, each racing to start their tasks.

Just then the door burst open, and Emil entered, carrying a black bag. He took one look at Fionna and dropped to her side, opposite Jasmin. Torie moved to lock the door, just as Max and Elric stepped through.

"What happened?" asked Max.

"That's what we are trying to find out," said Torie, locking the door behind the two werewolves. "Elric, can you call Glen? Let her know what's going on...even though we don't actually know the answer to that. We just need to let her know."

He nodded and walked away from the chaos, his phone to his ear.

Torie returned her attention to Fionna in time to hear Emil speaking.

"What have you found?"

"Nothing," said Jasmin. "It's like she's in there, but I can't reach her with my magic, and she can't reach me." She turned her attention to Torie. "Can you communicate with her? The way you can read the minds of shifters?"

Torie closed her eyes, focusing on her magic as she pushed her way into Fionna's mind. She felt no resistance, no struggle from the squirrel shifter. As a matter of fact, there was nothing. It felt like someone had reached inside her friend and plucked out everything that made her who she was.

"Nothing. I can't feel anything inside her," Torie stated. "Is she...?"

Emil's head snapped up. "No. She is alive. Her heartbeat is strong, but it is slowing."

"What does that mean?" said Jasmin, her voice more frantic than usual.

"It means we need to undo whatever was done to her. And quickly. Max, anything?" Emil said.

Torie and Jasmin turned their attention to the werewolf. Neither had noticed that he had been crouched near the floor examining every inch of the area around the door.

"If someone came in this way, I can't pick up their scent," he said.

Emil was nodding as he studied Fionna. "Just like at the scene on Cone Bluff. There was no trace of anyone there either."

Now it was Max who was nodding. "It's as if someone has figured out a way to mask their presence from wolf senses."

"And magic I'd bet," said Emil, with a slight nod in Torie's direction.

Torie stretched forth her hand, blanketing the bakery in a magical probe. "You're right. I'm not getting any pings anywhere. If this was a magical attack, I can't feel it."

Emil stared at them. "And the only people I know capable of doing something like this, and not leaving a magical trace, would be..."

"Hedge witches," said Jasmin, finishing his thought.

Immediately Torie's eyes blazed orange. "I will make them sorry for the day they even heard of Singing Falls."

There was a frantic knocking at the door, the banging relentless. Max opened it, and Glen raced through, running to her wife's side.

"Oh no!" she cried.

"She's going to be okay," said Emil, his voice hardened and filled with promise. "But we need to get her to my office. Now." He looked up at Max and Elric. "Can you help get her into the back of Max's truck?"

Instantly, the wolves were at her side, carefully lifting her off the floor. They made their way through the doors, with Glen close behind them.

Torie and Jasmin were headed for Torie's car when Max called out to them.

"Where are you going?"

"Where do you think?" Torie answered, clicking the fob to unlock the doors. She turned and faced the sheriff. "You and Elric watch over this place and one of you stay with Fionna until we get back. I don't want them making another attempt at hurting her or those kids in there." She gave

Jasmin a grim nod. "It's time we have another conversation with our friends over in Crest Haven."

In the early morning light, the mansion was as intimidating as ever. Torie's large sedan came to a screeching halt just outside the steps leading to the massive double doors.

"Just remember, we need answers. We can't go in guns blazing," said Jasmin as they climbed out of the car.

Torie slammed her door shut. "Whatever happens will be entirely dependent on the answers they give us, because these guns are locked and loaded."

They made it up three steps before the doors were flung open and several members of the coven streamed out onto the porch. Among them was the giant who had been guarding the door the previous night. There was a look of rage on his face and his massive hands were clutched into trembling fists.

Wands at the ready, the hedge coven leveled hatred at Jasmin and Torie. So much so that the two hex witches were momentarily taken aback.

"How dare you," said a voice.

Torie recognized her as the woman who had been vocal against them the night before. Next to her stood the man who had been equally as vocal.

Torie took a deep breath and stood her ground, refusing to back off the steps. "What is going on here? Where is Eliza? We need to speak with her."

"You are not welcome here," said the man. There was an angry murmur of agreement that passed through the coven. A wave of forceful magic rippled out, washing over Torie and Jasmin. With a wave of their hands, the witches brushed aside the coven's attempt at knocking them backwards.

Torie responded by summoning her own power and channeling magic into her hands. "I don't know what is going on here, but we need to speak with Eliza. And we aren't taking no for an answer. Our friend has been hurt, and I want to know why."

The man took a step forward, but a hand on his shoulder stopped him. Malena stepped from behind him to face Torie and Jasmin.

"You have some nerve coming back here," she said.

Torie frowned, recognizing the same look of rage and sorrow that they had seen when attempting to speak with her through the charm. "Our friend has been injured. We have reason to believe hedge witch magic was involved."

Anger coursed through Malena and her voice trembled when she spoke. "Hurt? And you think my mother had something to do with that? Is that why you killed her?"

Torie and Jasmin froze as the shock of the young woman's words washed over them.

"Malena...what are you talking about?" asked Jasmin. "We had no idea."

Again, a rush of anger moved through the coven.

Torie frowned at the woman. "Do you think we had something to do with that? Because we didn't."

"I am so sorry for your loss, Malena, but why do you think we had anything to do with that?" asked Jasmin.

Malena didn't take her eyes off Torie as she answered. "Because she was burned by a fire that was hot enough to turn her to ash but do no damage to her surroundings. Magic fire."

Her words caused Torie's face to go crimson as her

magic shimmered and faded away. "I had nothing to do with this."

Malena stared at her. "And yet you are here ready to accuse us of doing something unthinkable to your friend. Were you prepared to believe me when I said we had nothing to do with that?"

Their eyes were locked. Torie's determined yet non-threatening, Malena's filled with sorrow and loss.

"We didn't do this," Torie said. "*I* didn't do it."

The man stepped forward, pointing his wand at Torie and Jasmin. "Lies! They threatened us with fire and then last night returned to make good on it." He took a menacing step forward. "There was a witness that saw you."

Now it was Torie's eyes that grew wide in disbelief and anger. "Who was this witness? We deserve the right to speak with them."

"He cannot speak. At least not in a way that you can understand," said Malena.

All eyes turned to the giant, but he was still staring intently at Torie and Jasmin. The giant opened his mouth, but only a growl came out. Then, faster than they would have thought someone of his size could move, he charged at the witches. He leapt down the steps, fists raised, and brought them crashing down on top of Torie and Jasmin.

Chapter Eleven

The blow was thunderous. Both the giant's hands landed just inches from Torie's head. Only Jasmin's hastily cast shield of protection had prevented certain disaster. Before the witches could gather their wits, the giant struck again. He roared at the two of them, striking out repeatedly, battering at the barrier protecting them.

Jasmin's eyes began to glow green and she gestured at the man, releasing a bolt of light that drove him backwards momentarily, sending him crashing against the staircase. He shook his head, rising to his feet with a roar that caused the coven members around him to scatter.

He gathered his feet, preparing to charge just as Jasmin moved forward, raising both hands to unleash her full power on the giant.

"Jasmin, wait," said Torie. "Look at his eyes." As the giant lumbered forward, both hands raised in attack, she nodded at the cold orbs. They were a rheumy, milky-gray, lifeless and unfocused. "There's something wrong with him. Drop the shield."

"Are you sure about this?" The pounding of the creature's fists against her wards echoed around them.

Before Torie could answer, Malena had run up to the giant. "Jax, what are you doing? Stop this, my friend."

With a single swing of his arm, the giant sent the girl hurtling. The sound of her crashing into members of her coven was accompanied by screams from others standing around them.

The giant known as Jax turned to face the coven, dead eyes focused on everyone and no one as he marched toward Malena. The young woman closed her eyes, turning her head away as his hands drew closer to her.

"Stop!"

Torie's voice rang out, filled with magic as she used her power to ensnare Jax. Her eyes glowed orange as she compelled the giant to turn and face her, leaving the hapless Malena to scramble away from him. Torie held up a finger, pointing at the giant, and then began to chant.

"By this spell, I hereby decree,
break his trance, setting Jax free.
Let this hold upon his mind,
be shattered now, and stay behind."

Magic snaked forth, creeping like a mist to envelop the large man, wrapping him in hex power and freeing his mind of the fog that had swallowed him. At first, he fought against it, clawing at his face and trying in vain to punch the vapor away. Finally, dropping to one knee, he gave in, breathing in the power and letting it suffuse his being.

In moments, his eyes cleared, returning to their normal dark brown. He swung his head about, clearing the last of the cobwebs as Malena slowly approached him, much to the dismay of the rest of the coven. Looking up at Malena, his face twisted into a mask of confusion and anxiety.

"Jax? You okay, big guy?" Her words were tentative as she reached out, placing a hand on his shoulder. "You're alright. You're among friends. Everything's okay now."

Sorrow flooded his eyes as he buried his face in Malena's hands. She patted the top of his head, bending forward to whisper into his ear. Then, motioning for the coven, she bade them to come over and take the giant's trembling hand and lead him back into the safety of the mansion.

Torie and Jasmin watched as he was led back inside before making their way over to Malena.

"Are you hurt?" asked Torie.

Malena slowly shook her head and inspected her arms and legs. "No, I think I'm okay. It could have been a lot worse than it was."

"Ah, youth," said Jasmin. "If I had been tossed across some steps like that, I'd still be lying there waiting for my back to tell me when it was okay to get up."

Malena's eyes hardened as she looked up at them. "Why did you do that? Why did you save him? You could have easily killed him in self-defense."

"That isn't who we are, Malena. I told you that," said Torie.

"We don't believe in using our magic to harm innocents. We will protect ourselves when needed, but we always look for a peaceful way out, when possible," said Jasmin. "And, thanks to Torie's keen observations, it became clear that your friend wasn't in his right frame of mind. Any idea what could have caused that behavior?"

Malena looked genuinely distraught at the question.

"No idea. Jax is one of the coven's most loyal defenders. He is unwavering and beyond reproach. He was beside himself with grief and anger when he found my—when he found Eliza." She swallowed hard, refusing to let whatever she was feeling show on her face.

Torie and Jasmin exchanged looks. Finally, Jasmin cleared her throat. "Malena, Jax clearly was not in his right frame of mind. And yet, you and your coven still believe that he saw Torie kill your mother. Can you tell us what happened?"

Malena sighed deeply and sat down on the steps. Her body appeared heavy as it sank down under a weight that no one so young should have to carry.

"My mother was preparing for the Greeting Of The Dawn ritual. It's a practice that coven leaders perform every morning to greet the new day and receive blessings from the Early Light. She was in the prayer hall alone, as usual. Jax was outside the hall doors and said that he heard what sounded like a scuffle coming from inside. He tried to open the doors, but they were sealed, and he could not budge them. Then, my mother began to scream and Jax threw all his weight into the doors, finally breaking through them. When he stepped inside, a figure threw a powder into his face, one that burned his eyes and blurred his vision. When he was finally able to see, he says that he saw someone that he recognized. And that person recited an incantation that cause Eliza to smolder and burn.

"He said that figure was you. And when he lunged for you, you created a portal out of light and stepped through it, disappearing."

A frown crossed Torie's features. "Malena, can I ask, how did Jax tell you all of this if he can't speak?"

"Jax communicates with a form of sign language that is

understood by hedge witches. It is unique to hedge story-telling and was passed down from coven to coven for generations. He was so sure of what he saw..."

"And this was early in the morning hours? But you saw us as we reached out to you through that charm," Jasmin said.

Malena was nodding. "Yes, but I don't know the extent of your powers. For all I knew, you had just committed murder and were reaching out to threaten my mother's successor."

"Malena, I know this is asking a lot, but can we see the prayer hall where it happened?" asked Torie.

Malena frowned as she considered the request. "Normally, that is forbidden. No one but the coven leader is allowed in there. But considering the circumstances, I think it would be okay."

She got up, rubbing at her shoulder and stretching it out before leading them into the mansion. They made their way down the long hall and past the doors that led to the library. Just beyond that, the hall ended and there was a door leading to a set of steep stairs that led down a curved stairwell. Tall, iron sconces cast dim lighting for the witches as they followed Malena.

"Where is everyone?" asked Jasmin.

"In the library," the girl replied. "Most likely plotting."

Her words grabbed Torie's attention. "What do you mean, plotting?"

"I mean, they are all vying for who will take my mother's place as the next coven leader, therefore gaining the lion's share of the power the coven possesses."

"Don't you think you should be in that discussion?" Jasmin asked.

She shook her head. "I'm far too weak to be considered. Unreliable magic and all that."

They reached the bottom of the landing and headed down a long hall that led to a single door. It sat ajar; the frame bent inward in testament to the strength Jax had used to break it open.

The only light sources in the room came from dimly lit sconces that cast an eerie glow on walls covered in large, heavy tapestries embroidered with intricate symbols and sigils. The air was thick with the scent of incense, a heady mix of sandalwood and frankincense.

In the center of the room, a large circular altar sat, surrounded by a ring of flickering candles. Dark green, velvet cloth covered the altar, and atop it were arranged bowls of salt and water, a bell, and a small cauldron.

Behind the altar was a raised, wooden dais with an ornamental seating cushion also covered in archaic symbols. Torie saw Malena's eyes locked on the flooring just in front of the cushion. The boards where Malena stared were charred and blackened, as if scorched by a fierce fire. The flooring was warped and twisted, with deep cracks and fissures running through it. The scent of burnt wood lingered in the air, a faint reminder of the intense heat that must have been generated.

At the center of the burn mark, a small pile of ash remained, the only evidence of the hedge witch's passing. The ash, fine and powdery and pale gray in color, clung undisturbed to the flooring. Aside from the scorched area where Eliza had been standing, nothing surrounding the area had been burnt. Even the cushions and an open book on the floor next to it were undisturbed.

Malena had her arms crossed, hugging herself in order to ward off the horror of what must have happened in the room. Jasmin placed a hand on the girl's arm and gave it a reassuring hug before walking over to the open book on the floor. "Was this your mother's?"

"Yes. She always had that book with her. I always thought it was her diary."

Jasmin peered closer at the book. "It's a grimoire, but in a language I don't understand."

Torie walked over and looked closely at the book as well. "The page it's open to has a date on it; two weeks from today."

"What do you think it means? Why did you want to see this?" Malena asked.

Torie let out a slow breath. "Honestly, we were hoping to find something that could help our friend. She's in some kind of trance and we can't wake her."

"What made you think we were responsible?"

Torie paused for a moment but realized if they were going to help Fionna, they needed to be as upfront as possible with Malena. They needed her help, and letting the young woman in on everything might be the only way to get it.

"Malena, there is something you need to know," Torie began. "We have a physician, a very specialized medical examiner, that works out of Singing Falls. He examined the body of Clive—your father—and found trace amounts of materials that are typically only used by hedge witches. The configuration was designed to burn the body when it came into contact with water, so as to destroy any and all evidence associated with the body." She trailed off, her words sinking in as her eyes made their way back to where Eliza had been burned.

Jasmin walked over, studied the area and looked up at Torie, nodding. They both had the same thought.

"What is it?" asked Malena. "Did you find something?"

"It's possible that whoever murdered your father, did the same thing to Eliza," said Jasmin.

The young woman stood frozen, eyes wide with shock and disbelief. Her body trembled with a mix of fear, anger, and confusion as she struggled to process the enormity of Jasmin's words.

"I mean, we can't be certain," Jasmin continued, "but it's strange that this—" she motioned to the ash on the floor, "—is probably what would have happened to Clive's body had we not stumbled upon it."

Her face was pale and drawn, the color drained from her cheeks as if by a sudden gust of wind, and when she spoke, her voice was small and jagged. "What do you need to prove it?"

"I hate to ask, but can we have a sample of the ashes to take back to the medical examiner? I'm betting he will be able to prove that we are dealing with the same materials found on the body of your father," said Torie. "And can I take a picture to send him as well? And lastly…your mother's grimoire. It might have invaluable information in it that could help our friend."

Malena didn't speak, only nodded. Torie held out her hand and summoned a small plastic bag, into which she began collecting a sample of the ash.

Jasmin had been pacing about the room, studying every aspect of the space. "Is there any other way in or out of this room? Maybe an entrance that no one else would know about?"

Malena thought for a moment then shook her head. "Not that I am aware of. And no one else in the coven would be allowed entrance. So, it's not like they would know."

Jasmin nodded, still sweeping over the room with her gaze. "Tell us about the two that seemed especially aggressive towards us. What's their story?"

"Michael and Seraph," said Malena. "They both, for whatever reason, believe they should be leading the coven. They didn't always agree with the direction my mother was taking us and could be vocal about it."

"And were they both accounted for during the time your mother was...?" asked Torie.

Malena frowned. "I don't know. We haven't asked anything like that. I mean, I guess we are all still in shock."

"Understandable," said Torie. "Malena, I'd like your permission to bring in a friend of mine to look into what might have happened here. He's a sheriff in Singing Falls and also a member of the supernatural community. He could help lead an investigation into what happened."

The girl's face twisted in thought. "I should probably ask the coven if that's okay."

Torie stood and gave her a long look. "Malena. This is a coven affair. But Eliza was your mother. And you said Clive was your father. That makes it a personal matter for you. I think in a case like this, you have the right to ask for an investigation, no matter what the coven might think." A thought struck her, one that she prayed was wrong. "If someone did target your parents, who's to say you're not next?"

The young woman's eyes grew large, and she looked from Torie to Jasmin. "Do you think so?"

Jasmin reluctantly nodded her head. "At this point, we can't assume anything or be too careful. And if what happened to our friend is part of this as well...and I have a feeling it is, then I'm not so sure you're safe here. This feels like a coup attempt to take over the coven."

Torie had her phone in one hand and was snapping pictures of the area while clutching the bag of ashes in the other. The flash of the camera drew Jasmin's attention and her head snapped around sharply.

"What was that?" she demanded.

Torie looked at her, perplexed. "What was what?"

"Just then, when you took a picture. There was something else I think I saw. Snap another."

Torie did as she was told, and Jasmin immediately rushed to an area to the side of the remaining ashes. Holding her hands out, she chanted.

"With this spell, I call forth the power of the arcane,
to see what is hidden, to pierce the mundane.
Let the truth be revealed, let the secrets be seen,
by the light of this spell, may all be revealed and keen."

The air before her sparked as the floor beneath her began to glow. Slowly, a symbol appeared, etched in the flooring in emerald light. It was in the shape of an elongated eye, with a mystic symbol etched where the pupil should be.

Torie gasped and quickly snapped a picture of the image before it began to once again fade from view. She was about to speak when she noticed the look on Malena's face as the young girl stared at the floor, taking two steps back.

"Malena? What is it? Do you know what that symbol is?" asked Torie.

The girl didn't speak but held up her arm, pushing back the long sleeve of her t-shirt. There, on her slender forearm, was the exact same symbol tattooed onto her skin.

She swallowed hard. "My mother placed this on me

years ago when I was a child. She said it was for my own good, and that one day I would understand what it meant."

No one spoke as Torie and Jasmin stared at the strange mark etched years ago into the skin of a child by her now-dead mother. The same mark that now rested at a pyre of ashes that had only hours before been the leader of a powerful coven of hedge witches.

Chapter Twelve

"This is ridiculous! Why are we letting them be a part of coven business? Especially when they are most likely the ones responsible for Eliza's death." It was Michael, the angry coven member who had constantly voiced his opinion about Torie and Jasmin from the moment they stepped foot on coven property, who was railing to the rest of the assembled coven.

"Michael is right," Seraph chimed in. "Remember what we were always told about hex witches? They despise competition and embrace only that which they can control. We are no threat to them, but clearly, they don't feel that way."

A murmur passed through the massive library where they were meeting. Most were nodding their head in agreement, while a few remained silent, still trying to come to terms with how they felt about the past few hours.

"Eliza would not want them involved in our affairs," Michael continued.

"You aren't coven leader, Michael, and you can't speak

for my mother." Malena's tiny voice spoke up, and the whispers of the coven died down to silence. "And as Eliza's daughter, I want to know what happened to her. And if that means accepting help from outsiders who have experience in dealing with crimes like this, then so be it. Once this is settled, and my mother's killer is brought to justice, then you can resume your machinations to take over this coven. Both of you can." Her eyes shot from Michael to Seraph. "But until then, our first order of business should be making sure no one else gets hurt or worse."

Michael narrowed his eyes at the girl, but a hard clench of his jaws trapped any words he might have spoken.

"And that is really the only reason we are here." Max stepped forward, his steely eyes locking on first Michael and then Seraph. "We want to make sure whoever is responsible for this pays for their crimes, and we want to make sure no one else falls victim."

He and Elric had made their way to the coven at Torie's behest and had already made a cursory sweep of the murder scene. Now the hard part began as they would have to interview everyone who had been present at the mansion in the hours leading up to Eliza's death.

Malena had been right when she said the majority of the coven would want no part of this. But for her mother's sake, she had agreed to do what she could to make things go as smoothly as possible.

Torie backed away slowly, looking at her phone. She had been texting Emil and Glen to get updates on Fionna. While she desperately wanted to be at her friend's bedside, she knew that would accomplish nothing. She was better off at the mansion, looking for any clues that could help them wake Fionna. She was certain there was a connection between the attack on her friend and the death of the coven leader. She just couldn't prove it.

Yet.

She watched as Jasmin stood off to one side, consumed with the book they had found next to Eliza's ashes. It was a standard notebook with a protective green leather cover around it. It was filled with pages of hand-drawn sigils and lettering that looked nothing like either of the witches had ever seen. That, combined with the strange, mystic symbol on the floor that matched the tattoo on Malena's arm, was all they had to go on. But every instinct the witches had told them the answers they needed to help Fionna were here. They just needed to decipher them.

A huge clamor from the coven caught her attention and she moved to stand next to Elric. "What just happened?"

"Max just informed them that we need to speak to each person individually to take their statements," he answered.

Max was holding both arms up, trying to quell the dissent in the room. "Look, folks, I'm not here to cause problems. The single most important thing I can do here is establish the timeline for everyone's whereabouts in the hours leading up to the death and the time immediately afterwards. Unless you were in contact with Eliza during that time, I really don't care what you were up to. And what we discuss stays between us."

"You mean between you and your witches," came a voice from somewhere in the room.

Michael laughed, egging on the responses.

"And why should we listen to...one of them," Michael snarled, staring at Max. "A wolf in human clothing."

Seraph laughed wickedly. "Oh, I don't know, Michael. The other one looks like he might be fun." She tossed a dark grin at Elric. "What color is your pelt? Wouldn't be red by any chance? Cos that's a personal favorite of mine."

Torie felt Elric stiffen and could sense his unease in the room as he shifted his weight from one foot to the other a couple of times.

"Oh calm down," said Seraph dismissively. "We don't do *that* anymore. Well, most of us don't at least."

Torie held onto Elric's hand, flooding him with reassurance and trying to calm his skittish nerves. She knew that it had taken a lot for both he and Max to confront the coven like this. It was testament to just how much they also wanted to help Fionna.

"Psst." Jasmin hissed in Torie's direction and motioned with her head to join her.

"What is it?" Torie asked in a low voice.

"Just got a text from Emil. He said he found something with Fionna we need to see."

Torie rushed over to Elric, pulling him close. "We have to go. Emil has something on Fionna. Will you be alright?"

The wolf nodded, giving her a weak smile. "If I get skinned, I trust you'll avenge me."

Torie frowned. "You really need to do something about your comedic timing. Cos now is not the time for joking." She gave him a quick peck and followed Jasmin out of the library and to her car.

"Did he say what he found?" Torie asked.

Jasmin shook her head. "He just said it would be better to talk in person."

"Wait up! I'm coming with you."

They turned in time to see Malena jogging down the steps towards them. Her eyes were hard, and the set of her jaw told them she wasn't going to be talked out of it.

"Malena, shouldn't you be here with your coven?" asked Torie.

"They won't even miss me. Truthfully, they'll probably be glad I'm gone. One less person that might draw attention from Michael and Seraph." She rolled her eyes, then locked on the two witches. "Besides, you said that I might be in danger. Well, if that's the case, I'm safer away from them than I am with them. At least until all this gets sorted out."

They couldn't exactly argue with that logic, but still Torie cast her a look. "Actually, I was hoping you would stay and maintain the voice of reason. Especially where Max and Elric are concerned."

Malena waved her off and climbed in the back seat. "No worries there. They might talk big, but deep down everyone in there is terrified of the two of you. They certainly aren't going to try anything with your wolves. Especially not until a leader is chosen through which our power can once again flow."

As satisfied as she could be with the answer, Torie climbed behind the wheel at the same time that Jasmin settled in. Firing up the engine, they made their way back to Singing Falls.

"So, is it true that your town is filled with other super-natural creatures that live in balance with the humans?"

Torie shifted her weight in her seat, unsure where the girl's question was coming from. "Who told you that?"

She shrugged. "Just one of those things you hear. Is it true? Are supernaturals out of the closet there?"

"That's not how we would put it," said Jasmin. "But for the most part, yes, all the supernaturals in Singing falls live in peace and harmony with one another. There are some humans who know the truth, and they are accepting of the situation as well."

"But who's in control?" the girl asked. "I mean, super-naturals are definitely the more powerful of the two, so do they ultimately control what happens in the town?"

Jasmin half turned in her seat to look at Malena. "If we thought that way, then there could never really be peace. We see everyone, no matter who or what they are, as equals. Isn't that how it was where you moved from?" It was meant to be a leading question, one that would hopefully get the girl to tell them more about their life before their move.

"No. It definitely wasn't like that. No one knew we were witches. And when they did find out, things would get messy." She turned her face to gaze out the window.

Torie glanced over at Jasmin, giving her a look that told her it wasn't the best time to pursue that line of questioning. So, she changed the subject.

"Malena, what can you tell us about the inner workings of the coven? Who might have had motive to kill Eliza?" Torie asked.

Malena didn't take her eyes off the scenery whizzing by as she answered. "I wasn't privy to all the inner workings of the coven. As I said, without showing my mother's flare for magic, I was pretty much kept at a distance. I do know that she was working on something pretty divisive within the coven. Something that had to do with the reason she ran from my father."

This was the first time she had mentioned her father, and Torie decided it was as good a time as any to ask her about him. "Do you know what it was that Eliza had planned? And what was your father's role in the coven?"

"He was the leader at one point. But then they had a falling out over...something. I don't know what it was. I was young and not particularly interested in their arguments." She looked down at her arm, rubbing the area where the tattoo was. "That was when my mother gave me this. We left the next night." She swung her head around to face the back of their heads and opened her mouth to speak, but then seemed to think better of it and resumed gazing out the window.

Torie had caught her movement in the rearview mirror and nodded. "What is it? Did you remember something?"

Malena shook her head and faced them. "No, not that. I was just wondering. Could you...no...never mind."

"What is it?" asked Jasmin, turning to face her.

"I was just thinking that maybe you could examine me. Maybe see why my magic doesn't work? My mother always said that either one takes to the life of a hedge witch, or one doesn't. And well...I obviously didn't." She squirmed a bit in her seat and looked away. "Never mind. It's a stupid idea."

"No, it's not a stupid idea," said Torie. "I don't know if there is anything we can do, but we can certainly talk about it later." She didn't need to look over at Jasmin to feel the disapproval in her stare.

"It's just that, our types of magic are very, very different," said Jasmin.

"Yeah. You're real witches, with real magic," Malena said, trying unsuccessfully to hide her disappointment.

Jasmin shifted uncomfortably in her seat. "Our magic comes from a different source, that's all. We were born with the ability to tap into it. But, as Torie said, we will be happy to help you if we can."

The rest of the trip was made in silence and soon they pulled into the medical office behind the hospital where Emil had set up shop. The sprite was waiting impatiently for them at the door.

"Come on, quickly," he said, rushing them through the hall. He gave Malena a cursory glance but didn't bother with little more than a formal face as he ushered them into the sick bay.

There, Fionna lay in a hospital bed, hooked up to a monitor with glowing numbers that occasionally gave off a soft beep. There didn't seem to be any change in her condition, her body was rigid, arms still extended in the air, face a horrible mask of surprise and fear.

Glen was at her side, face red and swollen from hours of crying. Jasmin and Torie gave her a hug before turning their attention to Fionna. "I had hoped she would be awake by now," said Torie, reaching out to grasp her friend's hand. Immediately, she drew back in shock. "She's cold."

Emil was nodding, his eyes filled with concern. "Yes. That's because she's dying, and I can't stop it."

Chapter Thirteen

"What do you mean, dying?" Jasmin demanded, her voice flooded with panic. "I thought you said her vitals were stable."

Emil was visibly upset as he continued. "And they are. But the thing is, they are diminishing. Her heartbeat is slowing, as is her respiratory rate. But that's not what I needed you to see."

As he moved to stand next to Fionna, Glen dropped her face to her hands and turned, walking out of the room. The doctor took a deep breath and lifted part of the blanket covering their friend.

Her veins had become black and were slowly creeping up her arms like dark ivy across the brick facade of a neglected cottage. They stretched up the sides of her torso and onto her neck as well. But the most disturbing were the ones that crisscrossed her abdomen, reaching across to connect in circles and patterns that caused the witches to take a second, closer look.

"Is that...?" Jasmin's voice trailed off.

"Yes," said Emil. "They are forming numbers on her body."

"What do they mean?" asked Torie.

Emil shook his head. "I was hoping you might have some insight into that."

"Wait a minute!" said Jasmin, reaching into her satchel to produce the grimoire they had taken from Eliza's murder scene. She flipped the book open and pointed to the last entry.

Torie's eyes widened. "Those aren't just any numbers. It's a date. The same one Eliza had written in her book. A date two weeks from now."

Now it was Malena who crept forward, eyes large as she took in the scene.

"Still think the coven had nothing to do with this?" Torie asked.

Malena didn't answer, but her eyes never left Fionna's frail form. Finally, she looked up at Torie, her eyes wet and threatening to spill over. "I don't know what to say. I am so sorry you're going through this, and I will do whatever I can to help make this right. I just...I don't really know where to start."

Torie exhaled slowly. "That makes two of us." She turned to the medical examiner. "Emil, there has to be something you can do."

Before he could answer, there was a pinging from the computer by Fiona's bed. He rushed over, looking through the notifications.

"I ran a sample of her blood, looking for anything that might not show up on a normal blood screen panel. When I realized nothing was off with her normal physiology, I started to look for something that maybe normal science can't pick up." His voice trailed off as he looked over the reports flashing on the screen. "Yes. There it is.. There are trace amounts of Ytterbium and Neodymium in her system."

"What are those?" asked Jasmin. "I've never heard of them."

Emil arched an eyebrow. "I would be surprised if you had. They are both rare earth elements found in nature that, in large doses, are highly toxic to humans and animals. But it looks like they have been combined, along with another substance that can't be identified, and introduced into Fionna's system. Ytterbium attacks the nervous system of supernaturals, causing paralysis, and Neodymium attacks the respiratory system, creating an inflammation of the lungs. That would explain the rigor state she is in. But it's the third, unknown element that is causing her to fade away like this. I need to find it."

"It's called Lutetium," said Malena softly. "It's a substance that bonds with a creature on their cellular level. It's causing the other two elements to burrow into her very DNA."

Everyone stared at her until Torie stepped close and put both hands on the girl's arms. "You know about this?"

She nodded. "I've never seen it done. I've only read about it in my mother's books. The final product created from these three elements is called Deathbane. And given the fact that she is still alive, I'd say whoever did this to her gave her a very minute amount. But...it's still fatal, just a slower-than-usual death."

Torie's eyes blazed. "And is there a reversal for it? A cure?"

Malena closed her eyes, her face pinched together in concentration. "I can't remember...wait! Yes, there is. My mother always said that in hedge witchery, anything that is done can be undone. And I remember reading about Deathbane that the cure is Silverthorn combined with something else. But I can't remember the other ingredient or how it's made."

"Where is this book?" asked Jasmin.

"It's in the library back at the mansion. There is a room where all the really important and dangerous scrolls are kept. It's in there."

"We can have Max or Elric bring it to us," said Jasmin, taking out her phone.

Malena stopped her before she could reach out to either of the wolves. "That wouldn't be possible. The book is warded by nature magic and can only be held and opened by the hands of a witch. A werewolf wouldn't even be able to lift it."

Torie turned to Emil. "How much longer does she have?" She looked at their friend lying frail in the bed next to them.

"Hard to say. Maybe four to six hours," he replied. "I'm doing everything I can to slow the process, but we need that cure."

"And you'll have it," said Jasmin. "It might be close, but it should be enough time for Torie to get there and back."

Torie stared at her friend. "What do you mean me? Aren't you coming?"

Jasmin shook her head as she moved to stand next to Fionna, never once taking her eyes off the squirrel shifter. "No. Take Malena and get the book. There is something I want to try that may help her. At least a little."

She raised her arms at her sides until they were parallel to the floor. Her eyes took on an unearthly green glow and her voice sang out, strong and sure.

"Elements of life, earth, and sky,
I offer up my spirit high,
to heal my friend and keep them whole,
I give my life, my heart, my soul.
As my energy flows and fades,
I pray my friend to be saved.
And as my power ebbs away,
my friend's life force will only stay.
I give this gift with all my heart,
that we may never be apart."

Power flared from the witch. Green, life-giving energy suffused her and moved to envelop the prone figure of Fionna as well until both of them glowed with mystical, life-giving magic.

"Jasmin, what have you done?" demanded Torie.

Her friend's voice rippled with power when she answered. "I am using my own life essence to extend Fionna's. Science has slowed her descent into the nether realm as much as possible. I will do what I can to help her along. But I don't know how long I can keep this up. So, you might want to hurry it along."

The trip back to the mansion was made in silence as Torie concentrated on the road rapidly being swallowed up as she pushed her car hard.

Malena led them to the library where Max and Elric were at a table interviewing coven members one at a time away from the main group. Elric saw Torie enter the room in a rush and started to get up, only to be waved off with a quick shake of her head as she and Malena practically ran into a room at the rear of the space.

Unlike the rest of the library, this room was far more utilitarian than comfortable. There were no windows, plush reading chairs, polished writing tables or gothic lighting. In the center of the room, three raised platforms were spaced evenly apart. Three giant books sat under glass domes on the desk. The covers were of a soft black leather with a large golden clasp that held the volume closed, almost as though it were guarding a treasure.

"These were never kept locked until my mother found out I had been reading them. She said they were not for novice eyes and sealed them with a spell that only the coven leader could access," said Malena. "Even I can't open them anymore." She moved to the middle platform and pointed at the book. "That's the one you want. It's called the Alchemicon. It contains the instructions for creating some of our most powerful potions, including Deathbane."

Torie reached for the glass that covered the book and lifted it upward where it stayed in place, held open by a metallic hinge. The book itself had no lettering on the cover and rested on a piece of red velvet cloth that stood out against the darkness of the leather.

She carefully reached for the cover and tried to push the clasp aside so she could open the book. The clasp wouldn't budge. She tried to pick the book up, only to find that she could not lift it, despite there being nothing visible that secured it to the platform.

"Wards," said Malena. "Told you, only the coven leader can read its words now."

"Yeah, well the problem with that is, a new leader hasn't been chosen yet. And with Fionna in the shape she's in, I don't have time to wait for that to happen." She closed her eyes, reaching deep for her magic and then directing it at the book. When she opened her eyes, they glowed orange with magic. "The first thing you'll learn about hex magic is that it is driven by our will and our intent. And since it is my intent to save my friend's life, I'm not letting any wards stop me."

The first ward she encountered was surface level and easily broken. But the seal on the book itself proved much harder to overcome. She held her hands in the air above the book and mimicked opening it, but to no avail.

"Well. That's some serious warding for a hedge witch," she mumbled, more to herself than to Malena. She thought for a moment, and then held both hands over the book and began to recite an incantation.

> *"Goddess of the moon, daughter of the sun,*
> *Hear my plea, let my will be done.*
> *Grant me strength and make me bold,*
> *That I may break through this ward of old."*

Light flared from her hands, striking the clasp and sparkling high into the air around them. Still the clasp held. Torie poured more of her will into the spell and gritted her teeth as she continued to chant.

> *"Powers of earth and sea and sky,*
> *Heed my call and come from on high,*
> *lend your strength and lend your might,*
> *that my power may break this ward tonight."*

The air around them crackled with renewed energy as power overwhelmed the last bit of resistance from the hedge witch wards. With a fizzle and glimmer of light, the clasp holding the book shut lit up brightly before dissolving into a shower of glittery specks that floated off into the emptiness around them.

"Wow," said Malena. "I didn't really think you'd be able to do it. My mother said the wards couldn't be broken."

Torie smiled as she lifted the book off the pedestal. "It was a lot tougher than I expected. I have nothing but respect for the power your mother wielded."

She turned, leading them back out the way they came. Elric was standing at the door as they exited, giving them both a wary look.

"Everything alright?" he asked.

"It is now," Torie said, holding up the book. "This should help us get Fionna back. How's it going here?"

The wolf sighed. "As good as can be, I guess. So far everyone has been pretty forthcoming in answering our questions. And most importantly, no one has lied. Of course, Michael and Seraph will be last, so who knows how that will go."

Malena frowned. "How do you know if someone is lying to you?"

Elric tapped his ear. "Wolf hearing. We can hear the change in their heartbeat. And people give off a very unique scent when they tell a lie."

Malena raised an eyebrow. "Good to know."

Elric squinted slightly at the girl. "Why? Something you need to tell us?"

She shook her head and offered a smile. "Nope. Just curious."

"Look, we need to get back. But someone here has to know something. Find it. I'll see you back at the house later."

And with that, they were off. The big sedan roared to life, carrying them away from the mansion.

"Hey, this isn't the way we came," said Malena, looking around.

"I need to swing by my house to get some supplies. Find the cure for Deathbane in that book so we can grab everything we need."

Malena nodded and flipped the book open, leafing through the pages. "That was impressive, what you did back there," Malena said. "Is it possible to teach me how to do that kind of magic?"

"Oh dear, I don't think that I could. We are born into our power. Much like you are born into a family of hedge witches," Torie answered, casting a quick glance at the girl.

Malena sighed. "Just my luck. Born into a magic that doesn't want me."

Torie fidgeted with the steering wheel, thinking of the right way to word her next statement. "You know, it can take time to find out who we are and what we are meant for. It might not seem like it now, but time is on your side. Be patient, and what you are deserving of will come to you."

Malena frowned, turning her attention back to the pages of the book. "I know. I know what I'm meant for. Sometimes, I just get tired of waiting. But soon, things are going to change."

Torie focused on the road. Something told her she should fish deeper with this young hedge witch, but her thoughts were occupied with how the life of one of her closest friends now hinged on an untrained hedge witch and her understanding of a stolen book of potions.

Chapter Fourteen

To Max's senses, the air inside the library was a heavy blanket of sweat, stress, and fear. Everyone they had spoken with had ironclad alibis for their whereabouts at the time of Eliza's death. Plus, none of them had the skillset to enter the prayer hall, let alone take out a coven leader.

None except for the last two suspects, Seraph and Michael. They were playing hardball with the wolves, not being particularly forthcoming with responses. Unlike the others, they had refused to be separated for questioning and told the wolves that it was either both of them or neither if there was a conversation to be had. They sat on the opposite side of the table, casually draped across plush reading chairs, their eyes locked on Max.

"So, what exactly is his role?" Michael asked, pointing to Elric. "I'm trying to figure out who's good cop and who's bad cop, but it seems like that one is neither."

Seraph leaned forward, resting her elbow on the table and her chin in her palm. "Maybe he's disinterested cop. His job is to make us so bored someone confesses to something just to get away from him." She batted her eyes in a faux flirtation with the wolf, as he rolled his eyes and looked away from her.

For his part, Max leafed through a few pages of notes he had been taking before addressing the two hedge witches. "It seems that everyone else can be accounted for, and they all seem to know where everyone was this morning. With the exception of you two. No one recalls seeing either of you."

"Maybe because we were in bed, fast asleep," said Michael.

"Maybe," added Seraph, playfully.

Max looked from one to the other before scribbling in his notepad.

"What? Aren't you going to ask if we were together?" asked Seraph.

The sheriff shook his head. "Don't need to. Neither of your scent is on the other, so why waste our time?"

This seemed to rankle Seraph as she sat upright, a sneer crossing her lips. "How rude. You can't just waltz in here and start sniffing people, you know."

Michael placed a hand on her wrist, restoring her sense of calm. "Don't pay him any mind. He's trying to get under our skin."

Max stared hard at the man. "Actually, I'm not. Because that implies that I'm here to play games, and I can assure you that is the last thing on my mind. As for Elric, he's not saying anything because while you've been mouthing off to me, he's been spending the last few minutes acquainting himself with your biorhythms. Getting a baseline feel for you, in a manner of speaking. Just like a lie detector would." He looked over at his friend and nodded. "Ready?"

Elric gave them a steely look and then returned the nod. "The boy is a little twitchy, but I have his base readings."

"Interesting," said Max, zeroing in on Michael. "Care to tell me what's got you so nervous?"

The hedge witch frowned, crossing his legs. "Don't be ridiculous. I have nothing to be nervous about. Something is broken in your friend's wiring no doubt."

"Be that as it may," said Max, leaning forward, "Where were you between the hours of three a.m. and five a.m. this morning?"

"In my room. Asleep," replied Michael.

Elric stiffened. "No. Something is off about that answer."

Max raised an eyebrow as he focused on Michael, while scribbling fresh notes in his notepad. "Care to revise that answer, Michael?"

The man hesitated briefly before sighing. "Fine. I was in my room, but I wasn't asleep. I woke at around four, because there was a...disturbance."

Max looked up from his writings. "What kind of disturbance?"

"I don't know. There are various areas within the mansion that are warded. Eliza spent the last few weeks putting them up. And this morning, something brushed against the wards. I assumed it was Eliza adjusting them. She had been doing that the last couple of days."

Beside him, Seraph flinched slightly, her body stiffening just a bit along her spine.

"Seraph, do you know something about the wards?" asked Elric.

She took a deep breath and shook her head. "No, but I felt something as well. I thought maybe it was just a dream."

"So, you were asleep as well?" Max said, scribbling in his pad.

"Isn't that what most people are doing that time of morning?" she shot back. "Well, at least most humans."

Max ignored the jab and continued questioning. "Tell me more about this disturbance you felt in the wards. Was it someone trying to break them?"

Michael shrugged. "I really have no idea. Wards were above my skillset. I mean, I can sense their presence, but actively working with them is something I haven't yet leveled up to doing." He gave Seraph a sharp eye. "It's something none of us should be leveled up to do."

Max watched the two of them sharply before probing deeper. "Do either of you know why someone would want to kill Eliza?"

That seemed to let some of the air out of them as they sank deeper into their chairs.

"No," said Seraph. "She might not have been the nicest person, but she was an amazing leader. She was the most powerful hedge witch I've ever met."

"Maybe a bit too powerful," said Michael, glumly.

"What do you mean?" asked Elric.

Seraph shot Michael a warning glance, her jaw clenched tightly.

Michael yawned. "Oh, please. She's dead. What is she going to do to us?" He turned his attention to Max. "Eliza was able to do things that she should not have been able to."

"What kind of things?" Max asked.

"Well, those wards for one thing. The way she could move them from place to place at will. She could also manipulate energies to a certain degree. Like I once saw her make an object disappear and then reappear in another place out of thin air. She could also be capable of creating constructs out of magic. Constructs that could draw magic from other witches. Stuff that we were always told was forbidden and beyond the abilities of hedge witches."

Max could tell he was aware that Seraph was staring daggers at the man, but Michael refused to meet her eyes. "Who was selected to be her successor?"

"It doesn't work like that," said Seraph. "In a hedge coven, the leader is the one who demonstrates the greatest power and the ability to focus that power through their coven. That was obviously Eliza. The leader's second in command, the next to inherit the mantle of leader, is the one who rises to that position within the ranks naturally. Who Eliza might have wanted it to be, is irrelevant."

Elric's ears perked up. "So, I take it from your tone, that who she picked wasn't one of you two?"

Seraph didn't reply but folded her arms like a child sulking.

"Again, it doesn't matter. We are the two strongest members of the coven. The title would eventually go to one of us, not that—" Max cut himself off before finishing that last sentence.

"To what?" said Elric. "Her daughter?" He didn't need his wolf hearing to tell that he had struck a nerve.

Seraph's eyes grew dark and cloudy as her lips drew downward. "I will never understand why she was so set on Malena becoming something she obviously wasn't meant to be."

Michael was nodding furiously. "That child could not perfect even the most basic of hedge witchery. She was useless. Yet Eliza was determined to make her into something she wasn't."

"She obviously did not inherit her mother's gifts," said Seraph.

"Do either of you think Malena would be capable of hurting Eliza?" Max asked.

Michael all but laughed at the question. "Seriously? That one couldn't hurt one of us, let alone Eliza. Plus, she had no interest in even being a part of this coven. She made it clear, especially to her mother, that as soon as she gets her inheritance, she was out of here."

Max had been writing and stopped mid-pen-stroke, looking up. "What inheritance?"

Seraph frowned and looked around, gesturing with her hands. "This one, of course. All of this and who knows how much else."

Max put down his pen. "You mean that Eliza owned this house?"

Michael nodded. "This one and a few others across the states as well, I believe. Old money. Very old. From her husband's side of the family from what I hear. But I couldn't say since no one in the coven ever met the man."

"And with Eliza gone, Malena is the only heir?" Eric asked.

"Only one I know about," replied Michael.

Max thought for a moment before fishing in his pocket and taking out his phone. He opened the screen, swiped a couple of times, and then showed them the picture of Clive. "Is this Eliza's husband? The one with all the money?"

Seraph and Michael stared for a moment then shook their heads. "No. That's the guy Eliza was hooking up with. He's the reason Eliza left her husband, from what I heard," said Seraph. She leaned in salaciously. "If you believe the rumor mill, Eliza embezzled that money. Stole it from her husband's family, then used coven magic to hide her tracks and move here where she established a new coven and a new life."

Max frowned. "So, neither of you are from that original coven? Is anyone?"

Seraph nodded. "Pretty sure the only person with her when she came here was Malena."

"Oh, and Jax," Michael added. "He's been with her forever. But you won't get anything out of him. Not only can he not talk, but he's not the brightest tool in the shed, if you get my meaning."

Max ignored the man's ignorant comment. "I'd very much like to speak with Jax, and I'd like you to interpret."

Michael rolled his eyes and got up. "Fine. At least it will be fast because that man knows absolutely nothing about anything."

He left them, retreating from the library, only to return a few moments later, a strange look on his face.

"Where is he?" asked Elric.

Michael gave them a slight frown. "I don't know. He never leaves his post, but he's gone. No one has seen him."

Chapter Fifteen

Torie arrived back at the medical bay with Malena in tow, carrying a large tome she hoped would save their friend. Glen met her at the door to the room, sniffling, her body gaunt, as if she had used up all her energy to produce the tears that were no longer coming.

"Emil said you were retrieving something to help her. Is that it?"

Torie nodded. "This is it." She held up the book, triumphantly, refusing to allow any negativity to enter her mind. She stepped past Glen into the room and gasped at what she saw.

The darkness had spread across nearly all of Fionna's features. The black lines had covered her face, leaving only her eyes untouched. Beside her, Jasmin still held the squirrel shifter's hand, pouring her magic forth.

"She's okay, Torie," Jasmin said, her eyes closed and her voice low and weak. "It looks worse than it is."

Emil stood next to the monitors nodding. "She's right.

Whatever she is doing is keeping the Deathbane from reaching deeper into Fionna's body. The outward manifestation is merely a byproduct of the Deathbane as it continues to try and find ways around Jasmin's magic."

Glen placed a supportive hand on Jasmin's shoulder and turned to look at Torie. "She hasn't left her side. Not for a minute."

Torie had a large canvas bag with her, which she sat on one of the rolling tables next to Fionna's bed. "Sorry it took a little longer to get back than I expected. We had to make a detour to grab a few things." She reached into the bag and began removing various bowls and folded bits of cloth containing dried herbs. "You wouldn't believe what the final ingredient was for the Deathbane cure." She gave Jasmin a wry smile. "Lunarwort."

"Well, isn't that just the lucky coincidence," replied Jasmin, still focused on pouring her magic into their friend.

"Lucky indeed," Torie mumbled as she set out everything she would need. She looked over at Malena who had been standing at the door, her hands clasped in front of her. "Come on in. You helped us figure out how to cure her, might as well be part of the action."

Malena looked around nervously before stepping closer to stand by Torie. "What can I do?"

"Read out the ingredients and how they are mixed, and I'll put them together. If there are any incantations, let me know."

"Do you want me to say them? I can do that," Malena said, hopefully.

Torie thought for a second, but then shook her head. "No. Leave that to me." She looked up, noting the disappointment registered on the young woman's face. "When the time comes, I'll start you out with some smaller magic that I can show you. But right now, time is of the essence, and I can't risk my friend's life."

Malena nodded, understanding that there was a time and place for everything. She began reading out the ingredients as if they were items on a grocery list. As she read them, Torie added the appropriate amount to a large, silver bowl. The last ingredient was the lunarwort, and Torie saw Malena's eyes grow large as she carefully stripped the leaves from the plant and added them to the bowl.

"Have you ever seen lunarwort?" Torie asked.

Malena shook her head. "I've heard of it, but this is my first time seeing it." Her voice was almost reverential as she stared at the unused plant rested on the piece of cloth. She reached out, carefully folding the cloth over the plant. "It's very rare. Don't want to risk damaging it by leaving it out."

"Thank you," said Torie. "Looks like that's it for the ingredients. What's left?"

Malena let her finger trail down the page of the book. "It says to recite the following incantation to bring it to life and give it purpose."

Torie frowned and stared at the page. "That's odd. This is an extremely intricate and powerful spell. Not something that most hedge witches would be able to cast."

"My mother wasn't like most witches," Malena said softly.

Torie eyed the spell and shook her head. "And neither am I. I think I'll try this my way." She moved to raise her hands over the bowl, only to be stopped by Malena.

"But you're supposed to follow the incantation as written. At least that's what hedges believe. There should be no deviation in spells handed down from coven to coven."

"Well, I'm not a hedge witch, and the only coven I

belong to is the one that includes these two women right here before me." Her eyes began to glow as she placed her hands over the bowl and chanted,

"By the power of the light and the strength of my will,
I call upon the spirits to hear my appeal.
My friend lies in slumber, her spirit in thrall,
confused by dark magic, unable to hear my call.
May the power of the earth, sky, and sea,
combine with my magic to set her free.
Let the darkness be lifted, let the light shine through,
so my friend can awaken, and be whole anew."

At first nothing happened, but then, a bubble of light formed around Torie's outstretched hands. The light grew brighter as the magic detached itself and floated down into the silver bowl, infusing the ingredients with hex magic. Smoke and light intertwined, whirling upward from the bowl in a funnel, making its way to Torie's stricken friend.

It settled, penetrating Fionna's chest, spreading through her torso and limbs, filling the woman with warmth and magic.

Jasmin dropped her own spell, standing up and stepping back as the room glowed with power. A flash of light so bright it made everyone shield their eyes emanated from Fionna's body. And then, everything returned to normal as Emil slowly walked over to his patient. He looked up, his eyes wide with wonder.

"What is it?" asked Glen, racing forward.

As soon as she reached her wife's bedside, Fionna opened her eyes and lowered her arms. With a start, she sat upright, the look of surprise and fear still echoing in her features until she recognized the woman standing before her and eagerly threw her arms around her, pulling her in for a bear hug that nearly broke Glen's ribs.

Not that it appeared Glen would have cared as her tears started flowing freely once again.

Torie moved closer to the bed, holding onto a noticeably wobbly Jasmin. "You okay?"

Jasmin nodded, a smile breaking out across her features. "I'll be fine. That just took a little more out of me than I expected."

Together they made their way to Fionna's bedside where the shifter broke her embrace with Glen to give them each a hug, pulling everyone in until they all nearly collapsed onto the bed in a heap.

"Thank you," she breathed into her friends' ears. "I owe you more than I can ever repay. You just saved my life."

Torie blinked back tears of her own. "Don't be ridiculous. You don't owe us anything. Your being alive and well is payment in full."

"Fionna, do you remember anything? What was happening to you?" Jasmin asked.

"I remember everything. It was like being in a dream, or stuck in a loop, where all I could do was scream for help, but no one could hear me. Everything around me was black and cold. I was starting to forget where and who I was." She looked at Jasmin and took her hand. "But then I felt you. I can't explain it, but I felt you touching me, holding me, anchoring me in place, and all I could do was hold onto that feeling with all my heart. You were my light in that dark place."

Jasmin just shook her head. "I'm just sorry I couldn't do more."

Fionna drew back. "Well, I—" She stopped and looked at Glen. "*We* are very thankful."

"Do you remember anything about what happened? Who did this to you?" asked Torie.

Fionna frowned. "No, it was all a blur it happened so fast. Someone came into the bakery before opening. I told them to come back in a couple of hours, and they said something. But I can't remember what. And then that awful darkness just swallowed me up."

Emil leaned in and cleared his throat. "I'm sorry to interrupt this, but she really should be resting a bit more after all that, and I need to run a few more tests." He looked at Torie and gave her a slight bow of his head. "Not that I doubt the efficiency of your magics, but I want to make sure there are no traces whatsoever of any remaining Deathbane."

Fionna's eyes suddenly widened. "What about the bakery? It must be a mess. And how are Tara and Nicholas? I must have given them such a fright."

Jasmin placed a reassuring hand on her shoulder. "You don't worry about any of that. The bakery is just fine, and those kids you hired are the real heroes. They called us immediately when they found you. We will keep an eye on things until you're back on your feet." She leaned in and gave her a quick peck on the top of the head. "Which better not be any time soon." She followed that statement with a nod to Glen, whose stern countenance told them not to worry about that.

They stood to leave, and Torie noticed Malena standing in the entry, looking down at her feet as she shifted her weight from side to side.

"Oh, how could I have forgotten. Fionna, meet Malena. She was crucial in helping us find and implement your cure. We could not have done this without her." She stepped aside, giving Fionna a view of the young woman.

Malena stepped forward, hand outstretched. "Hello. I'm sorry we are meeting under these circumstances."

Fionna gave her a smile and reached to take her hand.

Before they could connect, a crash like thunder shook the room as the doors to the outer waiting area exploded inward. Everyone jumped at the noise and spun to see Jax barreling down on them, the room shaking with each impossibly heavy step the giant took.

He lurched through the door into the medical room, his massive shoulders knocking the door frames ajar. He looked around, eyes once again gray and dead, until they locked in on Malena. Without a sound, he moved towards her, arms outstretched.

His lips parted and a sour wind escaped his mouth. The wind echoed in the small room, the sound forming drawn out, twisted words. "Must protect," he slurred.

"What the...I thought he couldn't speak," said Jasmin.

"He...he can't," said Malena as she started backpedaling away from the hands that could encapsulate her entire head. "Jax stop...what are you doing?"

Still the giant continued moving towards her until a small diminutive body stepped between them.

"Get out of here," Emil said over his shoulder to Malena. Then, he held up a hand in the giant's face. "Listen to me my friend, there is nothing that—"

A single swipe of the man's arm sent Emil flying to crash into the wall away from the group. Malena screamed at the sight and fell backwards on her haunches.

Torie stooped forward, her hands glowing as she held them up. "Jax, whatever is going on, you need to stop before you make me do something we will both regret."

He wheeled on the witch. "Must protect," the sour wind repeated. He held up his arms, hands balled into fists.

Before either of them could act, a dark blur entered the room, leaping over Torie's head. Elric rose to a standing position, shifting from wolf to hybrid form. He turned and shouted at Torie. "Get everyone out of here!"

And then he leapt at the giant. Claws open and razor-sharp teeth snapping at the air.

Chapter Sixteen

Torie was shocked to see the wolf and hesitated briefly. "Elric? What are you doing here?"

The giant lunged for the wolf with surprising speed before he could answer. Ducking under his arms, Elric leapt on the man's back, reaching around him to pull his arms back. "Get them out of here." His words were little more than a grimace as he struggled to try and control the giant.

Glen was shielding Fionna's body with her own, even as Fionna screamed for her to help Emil. The doctor appeared unconscious, crumpled on the floor where he had collided with the wall. Reluctantly, Glen moved from the hospital bed and rushed past Elric and Jax to get to the sprite. She placed two fingers against the side of his neck and breathed a sigh of relief.

Torie watched as Glen carefully began to rub her knuckles across Emil's sternum, trying to stimulate consciousness. She moved to help but was cut off by a flying tray table thrown by Elric. She saw it strike the giant and ricochet in her direction just in time to duck out of the way.

Elric was right. His fight with the giant in such a closed room could accidentally kill someone.

She looked to Jasmin and could see her friend struggling to summon enough magic to help, but to no avail. Glimmering green orbs appeared around her fists but would quickly flicker and fade away, leaving Jasmin gasping for breath. She looked up at Torie, eyes wide, and shook her head.

A howl from Elric captured her attention and she looked up to see the giant had him in a bear hug and was intent on squeezing the life out of the wolf. Elric responded by striking the man with his elbow, dropping blow after blow on top of the giant's head until he released him. As soon as Elric hit the floor, he blurred forward, latching onto Jax's thigh with his powerful jaws.

Torie turned away as Jax began to pummel her boyfriend's back, trying desperately to break his hold. She closed her eyes briefly and called to her magic. Pointing her hands in different directions, she cast it forward in two orange clouds. One that enveloped Fionna and Jasmin, and the other that covered Emil and Glen.

Once they were bathed in her magic, she gestured, carrying them away from the melee and through the crashed door into the safety of the waiting area.

Then she turned her attention back to the two supernaturals destroying the room. Malena was cowering in the corner away from them, and Torie could see the terror in the girl's eyes. She reached out with her magic to cover the girl and pull her to safety.

But as soon as her glowing power enveloped Malena, Jax let loose a roar that shook the room. A savage kick dislodged Elric and sent the wolf scrambling. Instinctively, Torie reached out to the wolf, cushioning his fall with her magic and saving him from crashing into the wall covered with monitoring equipment at the far corner of the room. It had happened within a split-second, but when Torie turned her attention back to the giant, her blood ran cold.

Malena was on her feet with Jax standing behind her, towering over the girl. One massive hand covered Malena's head. With barely any effort, the giant closed his hand enough around her skull to make the young woman scream.

Torie took a step back, dropping her magic and offering up a plea to the giant. "No, stop. Don't hurt her. What do you want?"

Jax didn't respond but continued to stare in the witch's direction with dead eyes. Then, he took one lumbering step forward, pulling Malena along with him. As he advanced, Torie backed up, moving from the medical room into the waiting area where her friends were cowering, well out of harm's way.

Torie saw the giant angling for the exit and knew that he was planning to leave the building. She called on her power, channeling it into her hands. As soon as Jax registered what she was doing, he pulled Malena closer to him, causing her to cry out in pain.

"Jax, we only want to help you," Torie said. "But I can't let you walk out of here with Malena."

The giant continued to advance, his hostage in tow. Over his shoulder, Torie could see Elric making his way to his feet. She backed away slowly, still trying to placate the giant.

Elric sprung into the air, shifting into his full wolf form, powerful jaws aimed at the back of the giant's neck. Faster than she thought possible, Jax swung around and grasped Elric about the neck with his free hand.

And in a single, fluid motion, threw the massive wolf at

Torie. Before she could erect a shield, Elric's body collided with her, sending them both flying backwards, and her into the arms of darkness.

Swimming back to consciousness was an exercise in pain for Torie. She tried to sit, but there was a calming hand on her shoulder, lightly restraining her.

"Ow, my head," she said, reaching gingerly for the egg-sized lump on the back of her skull and wincing from the light touch. "How long was I out?"

"Not long." It was Elric. He was on one side of her, while Emil was on the other.

The doctor had her wrist in his hand, fingers on her pulse, while simultaneously staring at his watch.

"Pulse is strong and stable," he said. "You took quite a hit to the head, but—" he tenderly took her face in his hands and probed her neck, then lifted each eyelid, "—there doesn't seem to be any signs of concussion or spinal trauma."

Relief washed over Elric as he closed his eyes, mouthing a silent thank you to whoever or whatever shifters worshiped at times like this. "I struck you so hard, and you were so still. I was afraid I had...really hurt you."

Torie tried to smile but it turned into a grimace. "Well, you didn't. No permanent damage." Memories of what had just happened came flooding back and her eyes grew larger. "Emil, are you okay? Jax hit you pretty hard too."

The doctor smiled at her. "I'm fine. I may not be very big, but I'm tougher than I look. Don't you worry about me."

Slowly, she sat up, using Elric's arm to rest against as her vision came fully back into focus. "Where's Malena? Did Jax hurt her? We need to go after them."

"He was out the door before anyone could stop him," said Jasmin. She was sitting in a chair against the waiting room wall next to Fionna. "The spell I performed took way more out of me than I thought. I couldn't go after him."

"And even though I wasn't unconscious, I couldn't leave you," said Elric. "I'm sorry."

"Don't be," Torie said. "He hasn't hurt her. If he wanted to kill her, he would have done so when he had the chance."

"Did you notice his eyes?" asked Jasmin.

Torie nodded. "Yes. Same as back at the mansion."

Elric frowned, and Torie explained what had happened when Jax had first attacked Malena, she and Jasmin.

"You think someone else is controlling him?" asked Elric.

"I do," said Torie. "Something just feels off about it. He's definitely on autopilot. But I didn't sense anyone else manipulating him either time. Whoever or whatever is doing it, is very good." She frowned. "Wait, what are you doing here? Aren't you supposed to be with Max? Did you get anywhere with the questioning?"

Elric recapped what they had learned from interrogating Michael and Seraph. "And when they told us about Jax being the only other person who had been with Eliza and her old coven, we decided to have a conversation with him. I thought that even though he couldn't answer, maybe our senses could pick up clues from him in response to certain questions. But that was when we were notified he was gone. Max stayed at the mansion and sent me to find you guys. Good thing I arrived when I did." He looked down, embarrassment flooding his features. "For all the good I was against that thing."

Torie shook her head at him. "Hey, none of that. We don't have time for self-doubt right now. There's a girl out there somewhere who still needs rescuing. Why don't you go out and see if you can pick up their scent? Maybe we can still follow them."

Elric nodded, shifted into his wolf form, and bolted for the exit.

Torie slowly made her way to where the others were sitting, holding onto Emil's stronger-than-expected arm to steady herself.

He helped her into a seat next to Jasmin. "I'm going to get some aspirin and water for both of you. You'll thank me for it later."

"Let me help," said Glen, following him.

"What now?" asked Fionna.

"Well, you're going home with Glen to get some rest. I'll see what Elric was able to track down and see if he can lead us to Jax," said Torie.

"You'll do no such thing," said Jasmin. "None of us are in any shape to go wandering off after a giant. We won't be much of a threat to him in the shape we're in. The best thing we can do is get some rest and try to figure out what is going on here. We know that dead body is directly linked to the coven. And now, just as we start to sniff around, the coven leader is killed. And that giant starts acting weird and out of character. You're right, someone is pulling strings but staying in the shadows. We need to figure out who it is."

"Exactly," replied Torie. "And we won't do that by laying around waiting for a headache to disappear." She again touched the back of her head carefully, wincing at the slight pressure. "By the way, how are you feeling?"

"Stronger," Jasmin replied. "I can feel my magic coming back to me more and more by the minute."

"And I'm feeling much better as well," added Fionna. "I'm ready to pitch in."

The two witches gave her a skeptical look out the side of their eyes, and Fionna frowned. "I'm a shifter. We are known for our recuperative powers. You both know that. Besides, as traumatic as it may have seemed, I literally just slept for a very long time. Other than the horrible feeling that my body was its own coffin, I feel great."

Torie sighed, flinching a little from the flash of pain in her head. "Well, first things first. We need to find Malena. Then we concentrate on flushing out whoever is behind this, and that means digging into the coven. Someone there knows something. We just need to give them the right impetus to talk."

"Well, Malena did say they are terrified of us," said Jasmin. "And maybe we can find something else in Eliza's book. And now you have one of their other tomes that definitely had more to it than just the nature magic that most hedge witches utilize."

Torie snapped her fingers with a start. "The book." She got up slowly, with Fionna's help, and headed back into the room that had just been demolished.

"Where is it?" she asked, combing through the debris where the table and the book had been. "I don't see it."

She saw the bowl in which she had enchanted the ingredients on the floor, with her cloth satchel lying next to it. She went through the bag and looked up at her friends. "Not only is the Alchemicon potion book gone, but so is the leftover lunarwort."

Chapter Seventeen

As Jasmin held Eliza's book in her lap, disappointment etched across her face, she spoke with a hint of frustration. "If this book is a grimoire, it must be the worst one ever written. I know they served two very different purposes, but still. Why would the book of potions have been so straight-forward and easy to read and this one be such a mess?"

Sitting on opposite ends of the couch in Torie's library, they were lost in thought, trying to decide their next steps. As Torie absentmindedly stroked Leo's spine, the little dragon rumbled peacefully in her lap. The air was heavy with the scent of sandalwood from the incense burners on the coffee table mingled with the heady aroma of freshly brewed coffee.

Torie looked up, her eyes flickering with determination. "There has to be something we missed. If we're to assume that whoever is behind this orchestrated Eliza's death and that of Malena's father, then we have to consider that they're after something valuable enough that Eliza was willing to die to protect it. And chances are, that something is in that book."

Frustration creeped into her voice. There was so much going on around them and she had never felt more useless.

"Anything more from Elric?" Jasmin asked.

Torie shook her head. "No. He was able to follow Jax's tracks to the middle of the woods, about thirty minutes from here, and then they just disappeared. He's headed back to the mansion to see if somehow they show up there. In the meantime, we need to figure out what Eliza was doing with this book."

"Well, most of it is written in a language we can't even understand. Even Google won't be able to translate this," Jasmin said.

Her words struck them both at the same time, lighting up their faces like a lightbulb.

"No," said Torie, "but maybe we can. We still have some lunarwort left."

Jasmin took a deep breath, pursing her lips. "We do need to test that spell. I'm just not sure this is the right time."

"There will never be a right time. According to my mother's notes, the Dream Awakening spell allows the user to enter magical constructs and see the underlying, mystical code that created it. It sounds like it would be perfect for something like this."

She cleared the coffee table, and Jasmin placed the book on its surface.

"In theory, it should work. The Dream Awakening will allow one of us to walk into the book and see what lies beneath the surface. The language it's written in shouldn't really matter. Or we could accidentally destroy the book."

"Why would that happen?" asked Torie.

"Well, we could inadvertently trigger a booby-trap or a self-destruct spell. You've seen how fond this coven seems to be of fire."

Torie raised her thumb and forefinger to her chin in concentration. "Good point. Maybe we should set up some sort of containment spell just in case. After everything this poor house has been through, I don't want to go through another round of construction. Besides, I'm running out of contractors willing to work with me."

"And maybe we send Leo upstairs and away from us while we do this," Jasmin suggested. "Not that fire is likely to hurt him, but we don't need him striking out and adding fire to fire."

"Very true," replied Torie. She called the dragon over and scratched him behind the ears a few times. "I need you to go upstairs. Go to your bed."

The dragon huffed and slowly began to plod out of the room, turning to sneak one last look at the two witches, giving them a begging glance to see if perhaps they would change their minds.

"Don't give me that look," Torie said, pointing towards the door. "Upstairs. I'll see you in a bit."

They watched the dragon lift into the air and lazily zigzag his way out of the room, heading in the direction of the stairs. Once she was sure he was gone, Torie turned to her friend.

"First, let's put some wards up, ones meant to keep everything in rather than out."

Jasmin nodded but then hesitated. "You do know that what we do will trap anything that happens in a contained area...with us, right?"

"We'll set a series of wards. A couple to restrict everything to this room and then a stronger one just around the book itself."

"Good idea. I'll set the ones around the room. You handle the book."

Torie watched as her friend set about her work. The efficiency with which Jasmin set her wards was always a joy to watch. She was so confident and sure of her power, and that came across in the strength and intricacy of the wards she raised. Magic flowed from her, weaving over, under and throughout itself, creating a safety net that shimmered to Torie's eyes, stretching around the boundaries of the room.

Turning her attention to the book, she began to replicate what Jasmin was doing, but on a smaller, more concentrated scale. She concentrated on the book before her, filled with a sense of determination and purpose. Taking a breath, she began to trace intricate patterns in the air around the book, breathing out incantations that meshed with the power she was generating to weave a web of protection.

"All set," she said to her friend.

"Same. Nothing will be getting out of here."

Torie went to the floor-to-ceiling bookcase crammed full of her mother's books and retrieved the one they needed. It was the oldest and most tattered of her mother's collections, and she was very careful as she opened the pages so as not to inadvertently tear them. "It's very poetic when you think about it. Using one old book of magic to crack the secrets of another old book of magic."

"No matter what happens in this crazy world, the knowledge and wisdom contained in the written word endures," said Jasmin. "It's our link to the past and, hopefully, our roadmap for the future."

They looked over the spell and nodded to one another,

heading out of the library and into the kitchen and the greenhouse to gather everything required for casting the spell. Returning to the library, they took stock of everything they had gathered.

"It's weird, there isn't a lot here," said Torie. "Much less than what the hedge witch spells call for."

"That's because they need a lot of help for their magic. They can't tap into what we can to power our spells."

Jasmin rolled up her sleeves and the two of them looked over the spell one last time. "You sure you don't want me to be the one to go in?"

Torie shook her head. "You certainly have a better feel for magic, and under normal circumstances I'd be inclined to say it should be you. But you're just now recovering your strength. And of the two of us, I'm the one who has astral projected before. If everything goes according to plans, this should be a walk in the proverbial park."

Jasmin frowned. "I really wish you hadn't just said that."

They took up positions to either side of the book and closed their eyes. Each took a couple of cleansing deep breaths to steady their heartbeat and focus their will on the task at hand. Once opened, their eyes glowed with magic as they focused on the spell.

Jasmin held a silver locket that belonged to Torie over a bowl cast from pure silver. "Remember, this is to tether you to this realm. If anything happens, concentrate on the locket to return to this plane."

Torie nodded. In her hand, she held the lunarwort. She opened her fist and let it float in midair, then began breathing an incantation around it.

> *"Flower of the moon, grant this boon,*
> *let the magic within your gentle light,*

heighten my power and enhance my sight."

The lunarwort began to glow, a subtle, silver warmth that cast gentle rays of light throughout the room. Then, the plant broke into pieces, each dissolving in a mist of sparkles that wafted down to coat the book lying between the witches.

"Looks like that part worked," said Torie. "Ready for the real test? Time to see just what the dream awakening can do."

Jasmin let out a deep breath and nodded. They clasped hands over the book and began to softly chant.

> *"Through the veil of slumber, heed my call*
> *and show me now, the magic that powers all.*
> *I ask that my vision be part of the world,*
> *where magic is visible and mysteries unfurled.*
> *Let me slip through the veil and see with new eyes,*
> *the magic that binds all of life's ties.*
> *Let me see the energies that flow all around,*
> *and be part of its way, both deep and profound.*
> *By the power of our will and the power of dreams,*
> *let me enter the world where magic does gleam."*

There was a flash of power that took them both by surprise, and for a second, Torie worried that they had indeed triggered some sort of booby-trap linked to Eliza's book. But then, as quickly as the flash erupted, it was gone, taking with it Torie's consciousness.

"Well, that was a bust," said Jasmin, looking up at her friend.

She gasped when she saw Torie's eyes open wide and staring at the book before them. The usual orange glow of her magical signature was gone, replaced with a ruby light that consumed her orbs.

Jasmin still held her friend's hands and gave them a gentle squeeze. "Torie? Are you okay?"

But her friend didn't answer. Jasmin could see her standing there; at least her body was. But the Torie she knew, the best friend she had shared so much with, was gone.

Chapter Eighteen

As Torie had closed her eyes and recited the incantation, a tingling sensation began to spread throughout her body. A feeling of weightlessness, as if she were floating in a vast, dark space, overcame her as her senses were cut off from everything around her. Then, a burst of light exploded in front of her, and suddenly she was surrounded by a swirling vortex of colors, each hue more vibrant and beautiful than the last.

Colors she had never seen before danced around her, illuminating the air with vibrant energy. Threads of the multi-colored light were everywhere, illuminating nothing but more darkness. She could see the very magic that wove through everything, pulsing with a life of its own. She could feel the very power of the universe. It was palpable, pulsing all around her. She struggled to control her racing heart as she was nearly overcome by the overwhelming sensations of wonder and awe.

Everywhere she looked, magic pulsed in the air. She

could feel it, reaching out, calling to her. Her head tingled with the power of awakening.

Concentrating, she forced herself to focus. The dream awakening spell had worked, and what she was seeing was the underlying code, so to speak, that made up the magic around her. That meant she was seeing everything that comprised the magic in her house.

And there was a lot of it.

But that wasn't what she was there for. She narrowed her vision, mentally calling to that which she sought. Eliza's book. And there, as if the magic were answering her, she saw it. Not the book, per se, but everything that went into the spells making it up. It was a jumble of threads and filaments. Like a ball of yarn that had been loosely rolled.

Reaching out with her own magic, she plucked at the threads, pulling them free of the entanglement. Each piece that came free floated away, forming a new magical symbol. They appeared to be the same symbols found at the scene of Eliza's death. The glowing embers of light that had briefly flashed before their eyes, illuminated by the strobe of their phone's camera.

Only this time it was different. This time, she could understand their meaning.

Most of what she was seeing were indeed simple, nature-based spells. Ones designed for novice hedge witches. Something exciting and flashy, but not too dangerous. But then, one of the spells caught her eye. A flash of silver that she almost missed.

Tugging at the thread, she had to push aside others that clung desperately to it; almost as if it didn't want to be found. But she was relentless in her unwinding, coaxing the thread into the opening and casting it upward to reveal its secrets.

And had she been able to gasp in her current form, she would have.

What stood unlocked before her was the same pattern they had found at Eliza's death. The same symbol as the tattoo on Malena's arm. Torie tugged at the thread, watching as it revealed its meaning to her.

This can't be true. I need to get back now. I have to tell Jasmin about it before...

But then something else caught the witch's attention. There was something pulsing in the corner of her awareness. Something that was beating in time to the rhythm of her heart, and she felt herself drawn to it. Ahead of her, power thrummed. She could feel the vibrations from it in the depths of her soul. She drifted, her mind flowing to investigate.

As she drifted, she felt something stopping her, trapping her like a fly on a tacky strip.

The wards.

She should have gone back, she knew. The wards were there for a reason. But still. The pulsing called to her. It was close...just a little beyond Jasmin's wards.

Torie gathered a swath of magic before her and formed it into a wedge, pushing gently through the wards, opening a space just wide enough that her consciousness could slip through. It tickled as she passed through the seam, like a cool breeze blowing across wet skin.

And just like that, she was outside the barrier meant to contain and protect them.

Looking around, she saw even more magic, but by and far, what caught her eye was beneath her. That was the source of the pulse she had seen. Only here, outside the protective wards, the silver was dull and sickly. There were pieces of black attaching itself to the magic. Like a hungry leach, anxious to feed in a place where it didn't belong.

It struck her then what she was looking at. The ley lines. The magical conduits that occurred in nature and ran through many areas where mystical power was abundant. Torie had long theorized that one of the reasons there was such a proliferation of supernatural creatures in Singing Falls was because of the incredible concentration of ley lines that flowed throughout the community.

She and Jasmin's houses had been built atop an especially dense concentration of ley lines. It's what permitted Torie to create a spell that allowed her house to become self-sufficient in so many ways. It was also why so many supernatural creatures felt so at home in their presence.

But there was something off about the lines. The flow of magic through them seemed imbalanced. Rather than a steady stream, it appeared to stop and start, struggling to make its usual progress. But that wasn't possible. What could possibly affect the power of ley lines like this?

Her head tingled as she felt a presence approaching. It snapped her out of her contemplation of the lines, yet she struggled to zero in on it. Whatever it was, it eluded her, slipping just out of range of her senses. It seemed to be drifting away, and she sensed that following it wasn't the right move. She should head back to Jasmin, then the two of them could investigate together.

And yet...with what she had learned from the book, she had a feeling it might tie together. What if this was whoever was manipulating things from the shadows? There was definitely a feeling of foreboding about it. If she could just get a little closer to the presence. Maybe she could use the dream awakening to see who or what it really was. She drifted a bit more, reaching out with her awareness to make contact.

Yes. There it was. It had made itself small trying to evade her senses. But to no avail. It was like a hole in the magic that swirled all around her, a blank spot in an otherwise brilliantly colored canvas.

She reached out with her magic, throwing her power around it to keep it from retreating further. Once she had it, she drifted closer, focusing her awareness to examine what she had caught.

Too late, she realized her mistake.

The presence turned on her, darkness reaching up with clawed fingers to grab at her, pulling her down, shrugging off her feeble attempts at defense. The voice that floated into her mind was cold and remote, the two words that were spoken devoid of any feeling.

"Got you."

Chapter Nineteen

Jasmin felt the ripple of change flow through her friend. She grasped her hands tighter, the silver charm working as an anchor dangled from her wrist as she squeezed both of Torie's hands.

"Torie?" she pleaded. "What's happening? Can you hear me? If you can, you need to follow the sound of my voice back to me." Her voice rippled with magic, but to no avail. Her friend's hands were limp in hers, cool and growing colder as they sat there.

She released Torie's hands, letting them drop to her lap, and took off the silver charm, holding it tightly in both hands. She closed her eyes, as if in prayer, and whispered to the charm. Wrapping it in an incantation that she hoped would draw her friend back to her. She opened her eyes to see that the only response was Torie's head had dropped forward, her chin resting on her chest.

"Torie, please," she said, standing to try and shake her shoulders, thinking that might rouse the witch. She reached forward to tilt her head back, seeking to lock eyes with the woman. But what she saw startled her to her core.

The light in Torie's eyes was gone. Replaced by the same awful, gray dullness that they had both seen in the gaze of the giant.

Jasmin backed away, refusing to let panic take a foothold inside her. Instead, she pulled out her phone and called their friends.

All of them.

It took what seemed like only minutes for the house to fill up. Elric and Max were pacing holes in the floor as they walked back and forth, watching as Emil and Glen completed taking Torie's vitals and assessing her physical condition. Fionna and Glen had been the first to arrive and had helped Jasmin carry Torie to the couch in the study, where she had laid waiting on the physician to arrive. Leo had found her as soon as Jasmin had made the call and parked himself in a ball next to her on the couch, his head resting on her stomach.

"Well?" said Elric, rushing to Emil's side as soon as the doctor had placed his stethoscope back around his neck and stood up from Torie's side. "How is she? What's wrong with her?"

Elric wasn't the only one as everyone else crowded around the diminutive examiner.

Emil let out a long breath. "Well, as far as I can tell, her vitals are completely stable. Unlike with what happened to Fionna, there is no trace of Deathbane poisoning in her system. From what I can see, she seems to be enthralled."

"Just like Jax," said Jasmin.

"But unlike Jax, she doesn't seem to be violent in any way," said Elric. "She hasn't blinked or moved since I've been here."

"Jax was being used as a tool, a weapon," replied Jasmin. "Someone was controlling him to achieve an end. That doesn't seem to be the objective with Torie."

"Or whoever did this just hasn't pulled the trigger yet," said Fionna.

Jasmin didn't respond. The thought of Torie being manipulated to act against her friends was a terrifying thought. One she knew had to be prevented at all costs.

Max narrowed his eyes, moving from Fionna to Jasmin. "Are you saying that at any minute Torie could become...that she could attack us, with all her magic under someone else's control? Cos if that's the case, is there a panic room or something like that we can lock her up in until this is all sorted out?"

Immediately, Elric was in his face, a deep, rumbling growl emanating from his chest. Leo's head popped up, puffs of dark smoke unfurling from his nostrils as his eyes blazed at the sheriff.

Max raised both hands in surrender. "Whoa, easy there fellas. I wasn't serious. But this is out of my wheelhouse. So, I'm open to ideas here."

"I hate to say it," said Emil, "But maybe placing her in a place where she can't harm herself, or any of us, isn't such a bad idea. At least until we can snap her out of this."

Elric started forward but was cut off by Fionna. The squirrel shifter stood, eyes flashing dangerously.

"This is our friend we are talking about. I have to believe she would never do anything to hurt any one of us. We are not locking her up like she has already done something wrong."

Leo sent a large puff of smoke into the air as he flapped his wings in agreement.

"Agreed," said Jasmin, softly. She walked over and

placed her hand on Fionna's elbow, calming the shifter. "No one is locking anybody away. I promise you that."

Fionna let out a sigh of relief, her body visibly relaxing. "Thank you, Jasmin. But Max was right about one thing. What do we do now?"

"Let's think this through," said Max. "First, what exactly were the two of you doing when this happened?"

Jasmin recounted how they had used the lunarwort to create a dream awakening spell and what it would allow them to do. After explaining that Torie had been convinced there was something inside Eliza's grimoire that could help solve all of this—and find Malena—Max held up a hand, stopping her.

"Maybe she found what she was looking for. Maybe she found *who* she was looking for and went after them. Would she have done that?"

"No way," said Jasmin. "She would not have gone off on her own, leaving her body defenseless."

"But it's not defenseless," said Elric. "She knew you were here. And this is Torie we're talking about. I wouldn't put it past her to tackle anything on her own if she felt it would save one of us."

Fionna nodded reluctantly. "You're right. And that's exactly why we can't let her do this alone."

Jasmin was frowning. "I don't get it. This doesn't feel like something she would do. We were both trying to break the code of this book. It would have told us so much about the hedge witches and potentially who killed Eliza and Malena's father. Something is off here." She looked up, eyes wide as a thought struck her. "The wards!"

"Huh?" said Max.

Jasmin moved to the center of the room and opened her arms in a circle around her. "We set up wards of containment around the room. Just in case there was a booby-trap or something linked to the book. The dream awakening spell we cast was only focused on the book, here inside the room. If something pulled Torie away, it would have left a mark on the wards."

She bowed her head, closed her eyes, and brought her hands together in front of her chest. Touching the tips of her forefingers and thumbs, she created a triangle and began to hum softly. Raising her hands, she opened her eyes and looked through the triangle as she swept the room, coming to rest at a place against the outer wall of the room. Frowning, she stepped closer.

"Yes. Here is where she slipped out. She cut an opening in the ward. Why would she do that? Unless..."

She dropped her hands and headed out of the room, everyone else quietly following. Making her way through the kitchen, Jasmin exited the French doors and wound her way around the patio to the outside wall where the library sat.

Holding up her hands, she made the same triangle shape and peered through. "Yes, she was here! There was something here that captured her attention, but I can't see what it was." She looked around. "Nothing seems out of the ordinary, at least not to my eye. But under the influence of the dream awakening, who knows what she was able to tap into."

"When you say she was here, what exactly do you mean?" asked Glen.

"Her consciousness. Her spirit, if you will. The dream awakening separates that from the physical body in order to immerse your senses in true magic. It shows you the world that exists around and between the one human's experience," said Jasmin.

"So maybe she got lost in this new world," said Glen. "Is

it possible she is just wandering around out there some-where and can't find her way back?"

"We were afraid that could happen," said Jasmin. "That was why we set up a failsafe. The silver locket we used was meant to be her tether. Just on the chance that what you described might happen. But I tried bringing her back with it. She didn't answer my call."

"What if she couldn't answer," said Emil. "Travel of the kind you describe is fraught with all kinds of dangers. What if something took her, cutting the tether in the process?"

Jasmin considered his words. It was something she had refused to allow room for in the back of her mind. Some-thing had lured Torie beyond the safety of the wards. She had no idea what that something could have been, but she also knew her friend.

"You could be right, Emil. But Torie would not have gone down without a fight. Dream awakening or no, she would have found a way to let me know what was happen-ing." And with that, she concentrated, summoning her magic, focusing it until her eyes blazed emerald. Magic overflowed in her voice when she spoke.

"Magic unlocked, that needs no key,
show me any signs, that were left for me."

With a wave of her arm, she cast her power wide, watching as it drifted across the back yard. She was rewarded when it intersected a trace of orange magic that floated like a lazy river across the lawn, through the fencing atop the massive retaining wall, and out into the woods.

"Bless you, Torie," Jasmin said, turning to her friends. "She left me a trail of breadcrumbs to follow."

Elric growled, already starting his shift.

"No," said Jasmin, holding out a hand to the wolf. "You need to stay here. Fionna and I will go."

"What are you talking about?" demanded Elric, turning human. "There is no way I'm—"

"Elric, she's vulnerable in this condition," said Jasmin, softly. "I can't be everywhere. There is only so much you can do with us; but there is no one I trust more to watch over her and keep her safe." She turned and faced Max. "That's why I want both of you here. There is nothing to say that whoever is behind this won't come back. For all we know, the hedge witches could be looking for a way to take us out, and this was just their first shot."

"We'll stay with her as well," added Glen, motioning to Emil. "Just to make sure there are no changes in her condition that we need to worry about. Anything happens, we'll call you." She moved over to Fionna and swept her into her arms. "Do I need to say it?"

Fionna buried her face in her wife's neck. "Nah. I'll be safe. See you soon."

Emil grasped Jasmin's hand in his. His eyes were warm as he looked into hers. "Be careful. I know this looks bad for the hedge witches, but whoever did this was capable of pulling Torie out of a spell the two of you cast. No hedge witch I have ever heard of is capable of that."

Jasmin returned his smile. "I'll be careful. Take care of my girl."

Chapter Twenty

Thirty minutes into tracking Torie, the forest canopy seemed to thicken overhead. As they traveled the trails deeper into the woods, the trees closed in on them, casting deep shadows that concealed potential dangers lurking beyond. They walked in silence, following the faint trail of magic visible to Jasmin's eye, their footsteps muffled by the thick carpet of leaves underfoot. The air was thick with the scent of damp earth and decaying leaves, and the sounds of night creatures echoed in the darkness.

They pressed on, Jasmin employing her magic to ask the vines and tree roots to pull themselves aside so the two of them could pass unimpeded. Fionna trained all her senses on the darkness around them, feeling for anything out of the ordinary that could present a danger to them. She could see relatively well in the dark, but even she was unsettled by the eerie stillness of the woods surrounding them.

"She's going to be alright, isn't she?" Fionna asked. It was the first words they had spoken since leaving the house.

Jasmin slowed long enough to catch a lungful of air with which to answer. "She is going to be fine."

"Are you saying that because it's a witch thing telling you that, or because you want it to be true?"

"I'm saying it because it's what I believe and because it *has to* be true. I refuse to accept anything different."

They continued, Jasmin focused on the trail of faint orange light shimmering before her. She tried not to think about what they could be walking into. This was a type of magic she had never encountered before or read about.

Enthrallment and subjugation spells were one thing. But snatching the astral awareness of a witch of Torie's power was on another level entirely. Emil was right. It was beyond something a hedge witch could do. Maybe she should have brought Max or Elric with her. Sometimes, there was something to be said for brute strength in certain situations.

No. She refused to let herself think like that.

Someone had put their friend in danger, and no matter what it took, she was going to make sure Torie was returned to them, safe and sound.

She sensed Fionna tense and turned to face her. The squirrel shifter had her back to the witch and was staring intently into the darkness behind them.

"What is it?" asked Jasmin. She trained her eyes in the direction Fionna was facing but saw nothing other than blackness.

"I'm not sure. For a second, I thought we were being watched. But...maybe it was just my imagination."

Jasmin thought back to when they were on the plateau to harvest the lunarwort and how Torie had the same feeling. "No. You're probably right. Stay alert for anything."

She turned her own attention back to tracking the

breadcrumb trail Torie had left. They moved in silence for another ten minutes before she stopped short, looking around in confusion.

"What is it?" asked Fionna.

Jasmin placed her hands on her hips, breathing heavy. "The trail stopped. Like, literally just vanished in midair. Right here, where we are standing."

Fionna frowned. "Isn't that what Elric said happened when he was tracking Jax and Malena?"

Jasmin studied the ground before her, trying to discern if any of the mystic tendrils she had been following gave a hint as to where Torie had been taken. But there was nothing there. As much as she hated the word, everything had come to a dead end.

She bit her lip in frustration, wringing her hands. "I don't get it. It's like they just disappeared into thin air with her." She fought the panic that threatened to rise within. "I...I don't know what to do."

Fionna looked at her, then glanced down at the forest floor. "Okay, you know way more about this than I do, but I'm betting they didn't just disappear into thin air. If that was the case, why come all the way out here to do that? Why not just do it from Torie's house?"

Jasmin nodded. That made total sense, and she was annoyed at herself for not thinking it. She narrowed and refined her magical senses, focusing her will on her eyesight. "There's still no trace of them. It's like the earth just opened up and swallowed them."

Fionna's eyes lit up. "Maybe that's what happened." In a flash, she shifted to her squirrel form and began to examine the floor from her new vantage point.

In her squirrel form, the world around her suddenly

changed. Her vision heightened, able to discern the slightest movements of leaves and the tiniest insects on the forest floor. She felt the texture of the earth beneath her paws, the softness of the moss and the roughness of decaying bits of bark. The scents of the forest became heady and more intense, as pine and damp earth mixed with the sweet scent of wildflowers filled her nose.

This new perspective opened up a completely different world to her as she scampered about, examining things in detail that would be hidden to someone towering above. But in this form, she had access to so much more information than even her eyes could find.

Her ears perked up, finding a vibration that somehow felt off. Moving around, she zeroed in on it, straining to figure out what it was. The tiny pads on the bottoms of her paws were picking it up as well. Just beyond the normal rhythm that she expected to be present. She felt the invisible network of roots and fungi communicating and pulsing with life, the normal heartbeat of the forest floor was strong here; but beneath that, there was something else. A thrum that had no rhythm. One that was continuous and alien to the life around it.

She shifted back to human form and turned to Jasmin. "There is electricity running beneath us. There must be an opening, a tunnel of some sort, beneath the ground."

Jasmin nodded. That was how they had disappeared into thin air.

She pushed the sleeves of her jacket up. "Stand back." Pouring her magic into the ground, she called out.

> *"From the earth below and the roots that grow,*
> *I call upon thee to reveal what's below."*

Slowly, the ground began to roll and twist before them. The earth moaned as it pressed upward in waves, the roots of vegetation pulling apart under the witch's command. In a matter of minutes, Jasmin and Fionna stood before an opening in the ground that looked like a thatched doorway leading to dark, unimaginable secrets. A breeze emanated from the opening, warm and smelling slightly of mildew and rot.

"Well, that's not pleasant at all," said Fionna. "And definitely not part of the natural order of things around here."

Jasmin raised her hand in the air, casting a ball of green magic around it to provide light for them. "Come on. Let's go get our friend."

They made their way through the opening, pushing aside wet roots and clinging vines as they pushed through muck that pulled at their feet. Fionna was right. There was a tunnel beneath where they had been standing. It was formed by something that had dug free enormous amounts of earth, with the roots of trees forming a natural wall and ceiling to keep the ground above from collapsing. It was just tall enough for the two of them to stand upright in as they walked, and Jasmin wondered how someone the size of Jax could have fit through the space.

"You okay back there?" Jasmin said over her shoulder.

"Yes. I am not overly fond of small, tights spaces like this. Unless I'm in my squirrel form, of course," came the answer.

"Understandable. Well, you're welcome to ride on my—"

Before she could finish the sentence, Fionna had shifted and scampered up onto Jasmin's shoulder where she perched, peering ahead of them.

"Alrighty then," said Jasmin, casting her light farther ahead.

They walked farther along, the tunnel getting colder the deeper they went. Jasmin felt Fionna tapping at her shoulder and stopped. "What is it? I'm not like Torie, I can't communicate with you when you're in your animal form."

Fionna leapt from her shoulder, shifting in midair so that she was standing as close to Jasmin as the space would allow. "Douse your magic. I can hear voices coming from somewhere in front of us, and I can see light as well."

Jasmin stared ahead. "I don't see anything." Her voice had dropped to barely a whisper.

Fionna squeezed in front of her. "Put your hand on my shoulder. I'll lead us to whoever it is."

Without her magic to light the way, the tunnel was pitch-black and Jasmin could feel her anxiety heightening. She forced her breathing to slow as her friend guided them on.

Soon Jasmin could make out the faintest of glowing light, and a few more steps and she could hear the barest hints of voices. Every few steps, the sounds grew louder until she could make out a man and woman having a heated conversation.

"...Not what I signed on for!" It was the man's voice.

"Well, it's too late to back out now. Unless you want to end up like her," the woman answered.

Jasmin felt her heart skip a beat. Who was she referencing? Inching closer they made out a break in the earthen wall to their right, from which the voices emanated. Slowly, Jasmin pushed in front of Fionna and inched through the opening, the two of them hugging one side of the space as much as possible.

"I mean, what are we supposed to do with this? This is

so far above our pay grade." It was the man speaking, his voice filled with exasperation.

"We've done this before," said the woman, "We just combine everything and recite the incantation. It should work."

"What about that? Where does it come into play? And why keep it here? She's a hex witch. She should be locked away in the mansion in one of the vaults."

"Yeah, well, do you want to tell him that?"

Hex witch? Jasmin's ears burned hot and before she could stop herself, she barreled into the room that had been carved off the main tunnel. Her magic blazed bright and powerful as she aimed it at the scene before her. Fionna was at her side, her little hands balled into tight fists as they both stared at what was playing out.

The room they found themselves in was created by the same force that hollowed out the tunnel. Earthen walls and a smooth floor with vines and roots crawling across the ceiling supporting naked light bulbs that glowed with a sickly yellow light, turning everything it touched a pale, dingy hue.

Crude furniture, including a table in the center of the room, had been fashioned from brown vegetation that pushed its way upward, creating rough surfaces and ledges. On the top of the table lay Malena, perfectly still and eyes closed. Next to her stood the two people who had been arguing about the situation they now found themselves in.

Michael and Seraph looked up in surprise as Jasmin and Fionna burst in.

"What are you doing here?" asked Seraph. Her eyes were wide, and she froze in place.

"I don't think you're in a position to ask questions," Jasmin answered. "And you've got until the count of ten to tell me what's going on in here before I turn you both into living shadows." She narrowed her eyes, her green magic pulsing to life.

Michael stepped back, throwing both hands up. "Whoa, just wait a minute. We aren't here to cause any problems."

Jasmin stared at Malena, then nodded to Fionna. The shifter moved to stand next to the girl, placing her fingers along the side of Malena's neck.

"She's alive. She seems to be in some sort of deep trance."

Jasmin huffed. "Now there's a surprise. That seems to be going around lately." She turned her attention to the two hedge witches. "Wake her up. And what hex witch were you referencing?"

Michael shook his head. "We can't wake her. We didn't do this." He pointed at the book on the table next to her. Next to it was the lunarwort from the medical center.

Jasmin leaned in towards Fionna. "Keep an eye out for Jax." Then she returned her attention to the hedges. "That book, as well as the plant you have there, were taken from us. Along with this girl. And yet you tell me you didn't have anything to do with it."

"He's telling the truth," said Seraph. "But you can't be here." She was getting visibly nervous, looking around the room. "You don't understand. We have a job to do here."

Jasmin sneered at them. "Where is my friend? I heard you talking about a hex witch. Where is she?"

Seraph and Michael traded looks before the woman shrugged and pointed to a group of vines that had pushed their way out of the wall to form a crude shelf. Sitting on it was the crystal bottle containing the good luck charm Jasmin and Torie had created.

Jasmin frowned, about to yell once again at the hedge

witches, when she noticed something different about the bottle. She made her way to it, squinting as she focused her magical sight. Upon closer inspection, the contents of the bottle wasn't the charm she had created. Instead, it was filled with a murky, swirling smoke.

Wisps of trapped vapors that glowed orange.

She gasped and jumped back. Reaching out with her magic, she touched the vial to confirm what she thought could not have been possible. But there it was. Torie's awareness was trapped in the bottle.

Jasmin turned on the witches, her power flaring. Her hands shot out, reaching for the roots growing through the walls and ceiling. She felt resistance as the magic that had crafted them pushed back. Anger fueled her and she cast the feeble earth magic aside, grabbing the tree roots and twisting them around the bodies of the two hedge witches. The roots pulled, securing the hedges to the walls. In an instant, Jasmin was inches away from their faces, her eyes blazing with green magic.

With a sharp nod of her head, the roots slithered higher on the two captives, wrapping around their necks. "Undo the spell holding her, or I'll snap your necks."

Fionna stood by, shocked at what she was seeing. Her eyes moved from Jasmin to the bottle containing Torie's essence, to the two witches. "Jasmin, if you kill them, you might not be able to break the spell holding Torie."

Jasmin pursed her lips, her eyes never once leaving Michael and Seraph. "You're right. I only need one of them however." She flexed her fingers, causing the roots to tighten, cutting off the flow of air going to the hedge witches. "Whichever one of you tells me what I need to know first, lives."

Seraph tried feebly to raise her arms, either to launch

an attack of her own or to claw at the roots that were slowly constricting around her. Her voice was tight and thick, as if she were choosing between speaking and breathing, when she finally answered. "Why would we lie to you? Please, you have to...have to let us go. And leave before...before it's too late——" She gasped, her eyes growing wide with fear.

No, not fear. Terror. More than Jasmin had been able to strike into her.

Jasmin turned and saw Malena rousing awake. The girl struggled to sit up, rubbing at her face in confusion.

Jasmin turned her attention back to the witches in her grasp. Michael was beginning to kick feverishly at the wall in an attempt to pull himself free.

"Please...go! Leave before he gets here," he managed to get out.

"Whoever you're talking about, he'll have more to worry about than me. Tell me how to free my friend and you'll never see me again."

Fionna ran to Malena's side, helping the girl to sit.

"Shh, it's okay. You're alright now," the shifter said.

Malena looked up at Fionna and then over to Jasmin. Then, her attention drifted to the wall where the charm bottle sat. "Is...is that...?"

Jasmin nodded. "Torie. But don't worry. Your friends are about to tell me everything I need to know in order to free her."

Malena shook her head. "Looks like someone was sending you a message."

Fionna froze at the girl's words. To Jasmin, it looked as if someone had dumped a bucket of ice water on her.

"Fionna? What's the matter?" Jasmin asked.

The squirrel shifter backed up. "Those words. Send a

message. That voice. It's the same as the one that attacked me at the bakery. It was you..."

Malena swung her legs over the side of the table and let out a long sigh. "Oh well. Looks like the cat's out of the bag now."

She turned her attention to Jasmin, her eyes black as pitch as they penetrated the very soul of the hex witch.

Chapter Twenty-One

Jasmin stared at the young woman as she hopped down off the makeshift table, dusting herself off. "Malena, I don't understand. What is going on?"

"Of course you don't understand," Malena said. "How could you possibly understand?" She gave Jasmin a mocking look and shook her head. "And to think my mother was once in awe of the two of you. Hex witches this, and hex witches that." Her tone was cruel as she gestured sharply in the air. "You guys didn't turn out to be so tough after all. Certainly no match for him."

Michael began whimpering desperately as Malena talked, drawing the girls' attention.

"And you two. You had one simple job to do. I even gave you the instructions how to do it." She jabbed her arm out and pushed up her sleeve to reveal her tattoo. "But you couldn't even get that right."

"Malena, please. We were about to complete the ritual when they showed up. We weren't expecting her." It was Seraph who spoke, her voice pleading.

Jasmin took a deep breath. "I'm going to ask again. What is going on here? Did you attack my friend?" She nodded in Fionna's direction.

Malena grinned. "Yes. That was me. I needed to get you and Torie's attention. Clive's body was almost enough, but I needed to speed things up a little." She turned her attention to Fionna. "Still not sure how you survived that. Even at a lower dose."

Jasmin swallowed audibly. "And Torie? Did you do that to her?"

Malena frowned, pursing her lips. "Not directly, no. I would not have risked bringing her here were it up to me, but I now see why he did it."

"Who's he?" Jasmin demanded. "Are you talking about Jax?"

Malena's laugh was disturbing in a way that made Jasmin's skin crawl. "Jax? Are you kidding? That slab of brainless muscle could never."

Jasmin kept her eyes locked on Malena, even as she slowly relaxed the magic holding Michaela and Seraph in place. She didn't know if they would help her or side with Malena out of the fear they clearly had of her. But either way, she had a feeling she was going to need to focus all her magic to get her and Fionna out alive.

Malena's head snapped in the direction of the two hedge witches as Jasmin was freeing them.

"Uh-uh," Malena said. "I liked them where they were." She flicked a finger nonchalantly and the roots tightened once again, holding the hedge witches fast.

Jasmin frowned as she risked a quick flash of her own magic. What Malena was doing was high level craft, yet there was no magical signature coming from her. How was she manipulating forces without using magic of some kind?

"Malena, I don't want any trouble here. We just came to get our friend," Jasmin said.

Malena took a couple of steps, trailing her hand along the vines that comprised the table. "See, now you've put me in a tough spot. No one was supposed to know what's really going on here until it...well, after it was over. So now I have to decide what to do with you." She stopped moving, cocking her head to one side, her brow furrowing. Slowly, she nodded. "Yes. That could work. If she'll do it."

Jasmin was certain she was the *she* Malena was talking about. The question was, who was she talking *to*? Her mind was racing, trying to lock in on what she should do next. She had no idea what Malena was capable of, and part of her wanted to attack the girl right away. Go at her hard and fast, then escape with Fionna and the bottle holding Torie's essence. But that didn't solve her major issue.

She still didn't know how to free Torie.

Given time, she could probably figure out a spell that would do it, but the only thing with that was, she didn't know what, if any, damage was being done to Torie from being separated from herself for so long.

No. For now, she needed to play along with Malena.

Holding up her hands, she attempted a smile. "Look. No threat here. I promise you. What can I do to make this right? All I want is for us to walk out of here with our friend. What will that take?"

Malena's head tilted slightly to one side. Jasmin couldn't tell if she was considering her words or listening to whatever voice she had been hearing earlier.

Finally, the girl spoke. "Here's the deal. There is only one way to get your friend out of that bottle. And you're not going to like it. See, I can't force you to do anything —" she glanced over at the crystal charm bottle, "—but something tells me you're being genuine with your offer. But first, there is a matter of taking out some useless trash."

She looked at Michael and Seraph, and the two hedge witches' eyes grew large with despair. They opened their mouths, either to plead or to scream, but neither happened, as the only sound that came from them was the sickening crunch of bone as their necks broke.

Jasmin's mouth fell open in horror.

"What?" asked Malena. "A second ago, you were ready to do it yourself." She gave another dark smile to the witch. "Unless you were bluffing." Her eyes grew wide in wonder. "You were! You had no intention of killing them. He was right. Deep down, your kind is weak."

"Malena, who is this person you keep referring to?" Jasmin asked.

"Oh, you'll find out. When the time is right." She suddenly spun her attention on Fionna. "I wouldn't."

Jasmin turned to see that Fionna had managed to inch her way to the crystal bottle. Her movements had gone unnoticed by the hex witch but had somehow attracted Malena's attention.

"I know what you mean to them," Malena said, her eyes narrowing at the shifter. "You survived once, but don't think I will hesitate to kill you where you stand if you so much as touch that bottle."

Jasmin nodded for Fionna to step away, then turned her attention back to Malena. "She isn't trying anything. Just relax. She is just worried about our friend. And I'm worried about her too. Tell us what it is you need me to do so we can end this."

Malena clasped her hands behind her back, body stiff and lips pursed as she stared at the witch. "Fine." She thrust her arm forward, showing her tattoo. "I need you to remove this."

Jasmin arched an eyebrow. "Well, I don't have a skin laser on me, so..."

Malena snapped her arm to her side, her eyes narrowing. "It's not a normal tattoo. It's magical. I told you; my mother gave it to me. I need you to remove it. That's what they were attempting when you interrupted." She thrust her chin in the direction of the two dead hedge witches.

Jasmin frowned looking at the two bodies. "If hedge witches are capable of removing your tattoo, then you have an entire mansion filled with them to help you. You don't need us."

"Now see, that's what we thought," the young woman replied. "But turns out, old Mommy Dearest was a little sneakier with the whammy she put into this tat than I was led to believe. We needed lunarwort to unlock it, which of course is the one plant hedge witches can't harvest. I mean, we know where to find it, but we don't have the magic that allows us to keep it from dying immediately when we remove any part of it. It doesn't recognize our touch. But that was where you came in. You were able to get it for us."

"You did that to me knowing Torie and Jasmin would have to utilize it to save me. And that would give you a chance to steal some." Fionna's voice was hard with dismay, and Jasmin again had to urge her to be calm.

Malena regarded the shifter with cold eyes. "I'm sorry, is that a question or a statement? But yes. That's exactly what I did."

"All of this was just to lure us into getting lunarwort for you? You could have just asked. We would have helped you, Malena," said Jasmin.

The girl cocked her head to one side, her face a caricature of mock surprise. Then she laughed again. "I don't think you would. Besides, we needed to see what the two of you could do. Oh, and there was also the matter of the book of potions that Torie was so kind as to unlock at the manor. It had another part of the spell needed to remove the tattoo but was yet again sealed by a spell that we couldn't break. But a hex witch could. So, I had Torie to thank for getting me that."

She gestured and a part of the root that formed the table detached, unfolding to reveal the book that had been at the medical center along with the lunarwort when Jax had attacked them. The root stretched outward and flattened, creating a floating shelf that held the tome.

"Malena, who is this *we* you keep referring to?" Jasmin asked.

"He's my friend. He wants what's best for me. Always has. But if you're unlucky, you'll meet him sooner or later."

Jasmin started to ask for clarification but thought better of it. Instead, she asked something else that had been on her mind. "Did your friend kill Eliza?"

A look of shock and hurt crossed Malena's features and she shook her head. "She was my mother. Don't be ridiculous. Of course he didn't kill her. *I* did that."

Fionna gasped. "How could you? Your own mother?"

Malena rolled her eyes. "You don't know what she did to me over the years. What she had coming to her was long overdue."

"And your father? Did you kill him as well?" Jasmin asked.

Malena took a deep breath, letting it out in a hiss. "No. Now *that* I had nothing to do with." Her eyes hardened. "But trust me when I say, as soon as I'm freed of this tattoo,

I plan to find who did that. And they will rue the day they were born."

There was nothing but genuine hurt and anger radiating from the girl, and despite herself, Jasmin felt a brief stab of empathy. "Maybe we can help you with that?"

Malena huffed. Whatever hurt she may have been feeling was quickly shoved aside. "The only help I need from you is for you to make with the mojo and get this thing off me." She let her eyes drift from Jasmin to the bottle. "Or whatever is left of your friend in there will get sent to a place from which you will never be able to retrieve her. Tick tock. You're wasting what time she has left with all your questions."

Jasmin swallowed hard and nodded. "I'll do it. But it would help if I knew what that tattoo really is for. To cast certain spells, we need to understand what we are dealing with."

Malena seemed to give this some thought before nodding. "Fine. It's called an arcane cuff. It's meant to lock someone's paranormal abilities and keep them from accessing their innate powers."

Jasmin frowned. While she had never heard it called that before, she was familiar with these kinds of magic seals. If Malena's own mother put that on her, she had to have had a very good reason.

"Malena, why would your mother put that on you?"

The girl smiled. "I don't see how that is pertinent to your being able to remove it. You said you needed to know what it was, and I told you. Now break it."

Jasmin held out her hand slowly and moved towards her. "Let me examine it, and then I'll see what I can do."

Malena thought for a second and then held out her hand, letting Jasmin grasp her arm.

Jasmin closed her eyes and ran her palm over the tattoo, feeling the intricate mystical cyphers that went into creating it. "Malena, this is high level work. It is not something a hedge witch, even one as powerful as your mother, could have performed."

"Oh, she definitely had help from one of your kind. That's why we needed a hex witch to break it."

Her words stung Jasmin. Her mind flashed back to everything they had learned about the hedge witches, trying to find a clue as to when Eliza might have had contact with another hex witch. She also pushed her magic into Malena, probing gently, to try and find what Eliza may have been so afraid of that she would use hex magic to lock it away. She continued to run her hand along the tattoo as she probed, slowly pushing deeper into the young woman.

Then she felt it. To her magic, it felt like pushing her hand through tar. Sticky. Black. Clinging to her in a way she feared she might not be able to shake off. It was something foul and terrifying, and it clawed hungrily at Jasmin's magic.

And even though the hex witch wanted nothing more than to retreat, she had to know what she was dealing with, and the only way to do that was to let whatever it was inside Malena continue to pull at her. Let it come closer. Draw it in just a bit more. Until...

Jasmin jumped back, letting go of the girl's arm, her eyes wide.

Malena grinned. "I recognize that look on your face. It's the same one my mother had when I was small. Before she put this lock on me." She cocked her head to one side, listening to a voice Jasmin couldn't hear. Then she nodded. "He says time's up. Remove the lock now or say goodbye forever to your friend."

Jasmin followed her eyes to the corner shelf where the

crystal bottle sat. Only now, there was something else in the room with them. Fionna screamed, jumping back from the shadow that detached itself from the wall. There wasn't much form to it, dark and smoky, the only distinguishing features being glowing yellow eyes and pearly white fangs showing from beneath a hood made of shifting smoke.

The shadow reached out a ghastly hand and lifted the crystal bottle containing Torie's essence.

Jasmin watched in horror as it began to squeeze the bottle, and the sound of glass cracking filled the room.

Chapter Twenty-Two

Before anyone could react, Fionna leapt for the shadow, reaching for the bottle. As she wrapped her hand around it, another smoky appendage appeared, snaking forward to grab the shifter around the neck, pinning her in place.

Malena cackled. "Oh, now look. We have two of your friends. Looks like I literally hold all the cards now." Her dark grin faded away as her steely eyes locked onto Jasmin. "Now, stop with the games. No more questions. No more magical probing inside me...remove this blasted lock or say goodbye to squirrel girl and your bestie."

"Okay! I'll do it. Just, let them go first."

Malena shook her head. "How stupid do you think I am? First, free me from the tattoo, and then I'll let them go. Maybe."

"No, I need a guarantee that you'll let them go."

"Well, you're not getting it. I might let them go, or I might have my friend kill one or both of them. You won't know until you free me. But one thing you probably do know, is that if you do nothing, they will definitely both die."

Jasmin hesitated only for a moment, then motioned for Malena to lie on the table. She then moved to stand next to the girl and the book which had opened to a particular page. Glancing at the book, Jasmin scrolled down the page, then leaned over Malena.

"Well, no wonder this was useless to Michael and Seraph. The ingredients are one thing, but these incantations that sealed the tattoo on you are inscribed by hex witches."

"And that's why you're here," Malena replied exasperated.

"You killed those two for no reason," Jasmin said.

Malena shrugged. "Not for no reason. They were incompetent and constantly jockeying to take over the coven. Sooner or later, they would have turned on each other. I just saved them time and took things to its inevitable conclusion."

"Where is the lunarwort and the ingredients?" Jasmin asked.

As she was saying the words, an opening appeared in the table and another root slipped forward, this time with a small chalice carved from bone sitting atop it. Inside the cup was a murky, green substance with bits of silver highlights sparkling within.

"It's all mixed and ready to go," said Malena. "At least they were able to do that part correctly."

"You know, this is probably going to hurt," said Jasmin.

"Good. I like pain."

Jasmin shrugged. "Well, then you're probably going to love this."

She held her hand over the thick substance in the cup and closed her eyes. Summoning her hex magic, she sent waves of green energy into the cup, drawing the fluid up and out of it. Then, moving her hand over Malena's arm, she commanded the liquid to settle over the tattoo, spreading itself thin over the length of the woman's tattoo. She sensed Malena flinching as the magically enhanced ingredients settled onto her flesh. Once it covered the arm, it transformed from liquid to a putty-like consistency, hardening slightly under Jasmin's magic.

Once Jasmin was satisfied everything was in place, she drew up her power and whispered words of power and magic into the air.

"By the power of the moon and stars above,
I call upon the ancient spirits of love.
With fire and water, earth and air,
I break the sigil, its power I tear.
Let there be no hiding, from senses most keen,
as I undo this spell, let their true self be seen.
Let their powers flow, wild and untamed,
as I unbound this sigil, let them now be unchained."

The air around them began to crackle with magic as the putty clamped to Malena's arm began to glow red. The woman screamed then threw her head back, jaw clenched so tightly that Jasmin was afraid she might break her teeth. She placed one hand on the young woman's chest to steady her and held the other a few inches over her affected arm.

Breathing more words of power into the air, she began to make a clawing motion with her hand and watched as the putty followed her commands, and slowly began to peel back from Malena's arm.

And just like a piece of silly putty pressed against a

newspaper comic strip, it lifted the tattoo imprint with it, removing it from her forearm. Once completely removed, the putty curled itself into a ball and quickly disappeared in a circle of green light Jasmin conjured.

Malena opened her eyes, batting away the tears caused by the searing pain.

"Did...did it work," she asked, her words slightly slurred. Her movements were languid as she tried to rise.

"I believe so," said Jasmin, noting that the tattoo was gone from Malena's arm. She glanced quickly over at Fionna, who was still being held by the shadowy figure. She gave the shifter the slightest nod of her head before turning her attention back to Malena. "I'm sorry for this."

"What...?" came the slurred response.

Quickly, Jasmin shot her hand out towards the shadow. A bolt of emerald magic flared like a scythe at the creature holding Fionna and her best friend. As she hoped, the shadow became even more ephemeral, the entirety of it becoming vaporous.

With no solidity holding her in place, Fionna dropped from its grasp. She shifted in midair, flashing to her squirrel form and managing to catch the crystal bottle that fell with her. Once the bottle was in her paws, she shot forward, running through the opening to the room and into the darkness.

"No!" said Malena, still reeling from the effects of Jasmin's spell.

Before she could act, Jasmin cast her attention to the book sitting beside her. "Infernis!" The power in her voice caused the book to ignite in a flash of orange and white fire. Then, turning to the young woman on the table, Jasmin struck her as hard as she could, the blow sending Malena sprawling back against the table. Again, Jasmin flared her magic at the shadow creature before it could launch an attack in her direction, driving it back against the wall.

In an instant, she was gone. Out the opening and fleeing into the darkness of the tunnel. She threw a ball of light before her, blasting away the darkness as she ran as fast as she could.

Ahead of her, she could make out Fionna, now human, waiting on her. The shifter clutched the crystal bottle tightly in her grasp as Jasmin approached. Together, they made their way back to the main entrance only to find it blocked. Vegetation and roots had dropped down to close off the forest beyond it. Behind them, she could make out a loud scratching, and Jasmin knew the tunnel was closing in.

"No time to be gentle about this," she said.

With a wave of her arm, she sent an arch of blunt magic at the opening, blowing away the blockage and letting the cool air of the outside brush across their skin. Together, they ran out into the open air just as the tunnel collapsed in on itself behind them.

Fionna looked about in the darkness, eyes and ears searching the shadows.

"Anything?" asked Jasmin, bending forward to place her hands on her knees as she gulped air.

Fionna shook her head. "I don't hear or see anyone following us." She turned back to the panting witch. "Do you think they are coming after us?"

Jasmin stood and turned around to move farther away from the tunnel, motioning for Fionna to follow. "We're not waiting around to find out. Let's get out of here."

As they stumbled through the dense forest, they clung to each other, their hands slick with sweat but neither let go of the other. Fionna led, and Jasmin poured all her resolve into her legs, demanding they pump faster. Every now and then she risked a look over their shoulder but didn't see any signs of pursuit.

"Can't you just magic us there, or something like that?" said Fionna.

Almost completely out of breath, Jasmin could only shake her head before stopping. "I wish. I've only ever done teleportation spells with Torie. Both of our magic working in tandem to make it happen. But you better believe that after this, I am going to be working on a spell for just that purpose. How much farther?"

"Not far now. I can see the lights on the house just ahead. Do you need a break?"

"No. Just need to catch my breath. Better if we keep moving. I'll feel safer once we are back in our own home surrounded by trusty wards."

They pushed on, through air thick with the pungent scent of pine and damp earth, the only sound was that of their ragged breaths and the crunching of leaves underfoot. The only good thing about the twisty, dark path they were on was the fact that it was lessening in difficulty. The undergrowth was thinning, and the near suffocating darkness caused by the dense canopy overhead was starting to break up, letting bits of starlight in here and there.

And soon, much sooner than Jasmin had anticipated, they were staring at the retaining wall capped with iron fencing that announced the backside of Torie's house. They trudged around the trails to the part of the woods that emptied into her side lot and made their way onto her porch before throwing themselves through the door and into the quiet warmth that greeted them.

Chapter Twenty-Three

The two of them stumbled into the house, slamming the door behind them. Jasmin turned to face the door, arms flowing in arches through the air as she wove an intense layer of wards.

"Fionna, Jasmin, what happened?" It was Elric. He had sprinted from the back of the house to greet them. Max and Glen were on his heels, all staring at the couple with eyes wide.

"We can tell you all about it shortly," Jasmin replied. "But first, can you and Max take a look around the woods out back? Make sure we weren't followed by anyone. Or anything."

Her tone told them it wasn't the time to argue. In a swirl of light, flesh became fur and the two wolves thundered through the kitchen and out the back of the house.

Jasmin turned to Glen, who had swept Fionna up in a hug. "How's Torie? Is Emil still here?"

Glen nodded, breaking her embrace. "He is. She's unchanged from when you left."

Fionna let out a sigh of relief. "That's good." She reached into her pocket and withdrew the bottle.

"What's that?" Glen asked.

"That's Torie," said Jasmin, taking the crystal and heading for the back of the house where the study was. She found her friend still in the same position on the couch with Leo curled up between one of her legs and the back of the couch.

"Glen said there is no change," she said to Emil. The little sprite had been sitting on a chair next to her, two fingers on her wrist while he counted off seconds on his wristwatch.

"No change," he answered. "But given the situation, I think that's a good thing." His eyes trailed to the bottle in Jasmin's hands. "Is that...?"

She nodded, holding it up to the light. She frowned as she examined it. To her eye, it appeared that the orange vapors swirling about inside were a little less bright than they were before. A little more tarnished. As she examined them, Leo lifted into the air and flew over to her. Placing the tip of his nose against the bottle, he let out a low whimper, his scales flashing through a rainbow of colors.

"We need to figure out how to reintegrate, and soon. I don't know how much longer she can remain in this state," Jasmin said.

At that moment, Max and Elric came tearing into the room, shifting back into their human forms.

"No sign that anyone other than the two of you have been even close to the house," said Elric. "Care to tell us what happened?"

She quickly went over everything they experienced since leaving the house. By the time she finished, all eyes were on the bottle sitting on the desk.

"So, any idea how to put her back in her body?" asked Glen.

"I'm still thinking about that," said Jasmin. "Malena hinted that it could be done. But we didn't get any details."

"What about that shadow thing?" asked Max. "You seemed to think it was connected to Malena somehow. Could it have something to do with this?"

"I have to believe it does," replied Jasmin. "The level of magic needed to do this is way beyond hedge witches. And that tattoo on Malena was the real deal. Whatever powers she might have were locked up tight by it. She didn't do it, so that only leaves whoever it was she kept talking to and hearing. I think it was the shadow creature."

"Plus, that thing gave off some serious bad vibes when it touched me," said Fionna. "And the way it cracked the bottle when threatening us…"

Jasmin was staring at the bottle, tentatively running her fingers across its smooth surface. "I can make out the cracks, but just barely. Whatever spell they used to trap Torie inside definitely affected the makeup of the crystal."

"But you can get her out, right?" demanded Elric.

Jasmin studied the bottle, her brow furrowed. "I think the trick is going to be getting the bottle open. The stopper is fused shut, it's now part of the bottle. That tells me that breaking the spell may be as simple as breaking open the bottle."

"But why would that shadow have threatened to break the bottle if that would have broken the spell?" asked Fionna.

"Probably because we were so far from Torie's body that her essence may not have been able to find its way back. She would have been lost forever," Jasmin answered.

"But with us being right here with her, she could find her way back to her body?" asked Glen.

Jasmin nodded. "In theory, yes."

Elric was shaking his head, becoming visibly more and more distraught. "In theory? Possible? I don't like that. You're leaving a lot to the unknown."

"We may not have a choice," said Jasmin. "We can't leave her like this." She knew she was right, but the thought that her actions might result in the loss of her best friend was almost more than she could bear.

"So how do we break it open?" asked Glen.

"Stand back," said Jasmin.

Bringing her hands together before her, she interlaced her fingers in an intricate pattern leaving her two pointer fingers free. Aiming them at the bottle, she wove them through the air, then separated her hands quickly and slapped them together loudly. The air around the bottle cracked, exploding in a shower of light.

But the bottle itself remained stubbornly in one piece.

Jasmin narrowed her eyes and concentrated. She spoke words of power into the air, infusing magic into a weapon that she focused on the bottle, striking the crystal with as much blunt force as she could muster. Still, the bottle held with little visible effect from her attack.

Max stepped forward. "You said that shadow thing was able to crack it, right? Maybe, instead of magic, we try this the old-fashioned way."

He swept the bottle up, clasping it in both hands. Then, he began shifting into his hybrid form and squeezed the crystal with all the considerable strength he could muster. His forearm bulged and his fangs gnashed together with the effort.

And still the bottle held.

Max shifted back to human, breathing hard as he inspected the bottle. "I don't get it. What is holding this thing together?"

Jasmin placed a hand on Elric as he paced back and forth in front of her. "It's going to be alright, Elric. We're going to fix this."

"Maybe we just need more force than we can generate," said Fionna.

"How about a gun? I can get my rifle," added Glen.

"Or maybe we can strike it with another enchanted artifact," suggested Emil. "Something made of pure silver perhaps?"

They all began talking, throwing out ideas of what could be used to break through the glass and free their friend. The din of their conversation was growing, and they almost missed the tiny voice that spoke out.

"Me."

Slowly the group quieted, turning to the source of the voice. It was Leo. The tiny dragon was sitting on the floor looking back at all the open-mouthed, wide-eyed, staring group of friends.

Max pointed. "Did that little—" he started.

"Leo," said Jasmin in a soft voice, "how do you think you can help?"

His eyes went to the bottle that Max was still holding. "Must help." His voice was low and ragged, guttural with just a hint of a hiss.

Jasmin took the bottle from Max and placed it on the desk. Leo's wings created the tiniest stir in the air as he lifted off the ground, hovering level with the crystal.

Without warning, the dragon drew in breath and blasted out a stream of blue fire directed at the bottle. In an instant, the flame grew from blue to white and Jasmin immediately threw up a protective barrier around herself and her friends. It was like standing next to a blast furnace as Leo continued to concentrate his fire on the bottle.

In return, the bottle began to glow as well. Heated by the supernatural fire, the glass expanded, giving off a groaning sound as it tried in vain to resist the heat being poured into it. Though the fire was directed in a small beam only at the bottle, the desk on which it sat began to warp and char, and books lining the shelves behind it smoked as residual heat threatened to cause them to burst into flames.

Just when Jasmin was sure the dragon's fire was going to burn the house down, the bottle shattered into thousands of flaming shards.

The dragon's fire was exhausted and stopped without so much as a puff of residual smoke from his snout. Without a word, he dropped to the floor, unmoving.

At the same time, the swirling mass of orange mist that was freed expanded in the air above the broken bottle before flowing into the unconscious witch on the couch. As Leo fell, Torie's eyes opened with a flutter, and she drew in a great, gasping breath. Her hand flew to her chest as she sat up, looking frantically about the space.

Dropping the shields, Jasmin hurried to her friend's side. She grasped Torie's hand, looking her in the eye. "Torie, are you okay?"

Confusion crept across her face as she looked around. "Where am I? What happened?"

Elric was at her side, kneeling on one knee as he held her hand. "You don't remember?"

She shook her head slowly, trying to clear the cobwebs. "No. I mean, I remember Jasmin and I were working on the dream awakening spell." She frowned, deep in thought. "And it worked. I remember seeing everything that was written in Eliza's book and being able to understand it. Then..." Her voice trailed off and her eyes drifted, looking at something far away. "Oh no! I remember! I was trying to warn Jasmin. Malena. She's not what we thought. But then everything went black." She sat up suddenly. "We need to—"

"It's okay," said Jasmin, calmly. She placed her hand on her friend's shoulder, urging her to rest back against the pillows. "We know about Malena."

For a moment, Torie's eyes went bright orange with magic. "I was trapped. He grabbed me and locked me away in something. It's all a blur but it's starting to come back to me. I remember screaming for help, but no one could hear me. I was starting to fade away, to forget who I was. It was terrifying." She looked at Jasmin, grasping her friend's hand. "How? How did you pull me out?"

"Well, as much as I'd like to take credit for it, it was Leo that did what we couldn't."

Torie's eyes grew wider. "Leo? Where is he?"

Jasmin looked towards the heap on the floor, and Torie followed her gaze. There, before the desk, knelt Emil. In his hands he cradled the little dragon. The doctor looked up, his face a mask of sorrow. "He...he's not breathing."

Chapter Twenty-Four

"I would feel much better if you would just let him give you a thorough checkup," Jasmin said.

"I am fine. Trust me. I'm more worried about him," Torie replied.

They were in Torie's primary bedroom, seated in two stylish wingback chairs facing the fireplace. Torie had moved Leo's bedding directly in front of the fireplace and the little dragon was curled in a ball fast asleep.

"He almost died saving me," Torie said, her eyes misting over as she watched Leo sleep. She looked up at her friend. "And so did you and Fionna. You risked everything for me."

"But we didn't die. And you would have done the same thing for any of us without a second's hesitation."

Torie didn't answer but returned her attention to the dragon. "Will his fire ever come back?"

Jasmin sighed. "Emil says there is every chance it will. Apparently, he just burned himself out breaking you free of that trap. He used it all up. But Emil thinks all he needs is time and rest."

The dragon snored peacefully, twitching his little paws from time to time to the beat of a dream that neither of the witches could probably ever imagine.

When she had seen him so limp and lifeless, Torie had panicked. It had taken Emil and Glen fifteen minutes to get him back to the point where he was breathing regularly again. And even longer than that to get him up and moving around under his own power.

Once he was roused, the dragon had sat, eyes blinking lazily until he seemed to realize where he was and recognize Torie. Then, with a single bound, he had been in her arms, his head nuzzled against her chest.

And for a brief moment, Torie had breathed a sigh of relief, and everything had felt right in the world. She knew it wouldn't last, but she had also learned to celebrate the little wins.

And being trapped inside a bottle and not dying felt like a win at the moment.

"So, I gotta know," said Jasmin, "was it like being inside Jeannie's bottle when you were in there? Did you have a wraparound couch with psychedelic wallpaper and throw pillows everywhere? Cause you know, when I was a kid, I really wanted to live in that bottle."

Despite herself Torie roared with laughter. "Thank you. I needed that. And no. It was nothing like being inside a genie bottle." Her eyes grew distant as memories flooded her. "Even though it shouldn't have been possible, I just remember how cold it was. Soul-numbing cold that I can't even explain. All I wanted to do was fall asleep just to get away from that cold, but I knew if I did, I would never wake up again."

In response to her words, the fireplace blazed with

crackling flames jumping higher. Leo cooed in his sleep and snuggled closer to the blaze, still in a deep slumber.

Torie picked up a glass sitting on a bronze serving tray on the large ottoman between their two chairs. She downed the last of the water, sitting the empty glass down and watching as the tray floated in the air and made its way out of the room where it would be washed, dried, and put away by the house's self-cleaning spells.

She sighed, sitting back in the chair. "When you were confronting Malena, you mentioned that she was referring to, or speaking with, someone you couldn't hear. It could have been the same creature I encountered."

Jasmin thought for a moment. "I assumed it was the shadow. But in all honesty, I don't know."

"And you never felt any power emanating from Malena, right? What about the creature?"

Jasmin's brow dipped. "Now that you mention it, no. One minute it wasn't there, the next it just appeared. But I never sensed anything. Yet, it had some type of corporeal presence, otherwise it would not have been able to hold Fionna against her will, or threaten the bottle you were in. Why?"

"The thing that grabbed me was the same way. There was no warning, no telltale sense of a magical presence. It was like it appeared out of nowhere and snatched me up. Who is able to do that?"

Her friend shook her head, reaching out to take one of the iron pokers and shift some of the logs around in the fireplace. "I don't know. Someone...some*thing*,new to us. With considerable magical abilities."

"And there was something else as well. I didn't just drift out of the warded zone when we were performing the dream awakening spell. I was lured outside. That's how it nabbed me. But, what I noticed, just before being captured, were the ley lines."

"What about them?"

"I'm not sure. They looked sick. Or contaminated. Something was definitely off about them."

Jasmin appeared deep in thought for a moment as she digested what her friend had said. "The ley lines are a natural part of the magic that flows in and around certain locations. They have been around since the beginning of time. The first witches tapped into them in order to perform acts of magic. The ley lines are the source of all our powers. The thought that something out there could be tampering with them is scary."

"Could that explain the blind spots we are experiencing?"

Jasmin frowned. "How do you mean?"

"Well, you just said that our power ultimately stems from the lines. What if someone else has found a way to use them as well? To tap into the natural source of magic that we get our powers from. Would they be able to hide their use of magic from us?"

"In theory, I suppose that could happen," Jasmin answered. "But aside from hex witches, there are very few others able to trace the source of their magic to the ley lines. How could someone like that be operating this close to Singing Falls and us not know?"

"Well, there was an entire coven of hedge witches in the next town over and we didn't know about them."

"We don't sense their magic unless it is aimed directly at us. The source of their power comes from nature. But it's not something they can tap into and use directly. They need outside conduits in the form of potions, elixirs, and other ritual."

Torie's eyes widened. "As far as we know. What if they figured out a way to bypass all that? A way to utilize the ley lines directly."

Jasmin was nodding slowly. "That could also be a double-edged sword. We might not be able to sense their use of magic, but they will have a built-in vulnerability to our magic as well."

"How do you mean?"

"Well, we were born into our magic. We can tap it directly with our willpower. But if whoever is behind this is just another hedge witch who has figured out a new way to access magic for them, they will still never be able to wield it the way we can. Maybe they can imitate what it is they think we do...but they will never be able to fully understand it."

"Or break it," said Torie in a rush. "That's why they lured me outside of your wards. They couldn't get through our hex magic."

"Exactly."

"Malena said that Eliza had put a ward around the Alchemicon, the potion book, that the hedges couldn't touch. None of them were capable of opening it. Maybe Eliza used hex magic to ward it."

"That's possible. But that would mean Eliza would have to be a hex witch to begin with. Why would she be working with a coven of hedge witches?" Jasmin asked.

"Either she is, or she had help. Someone else who is a hex witch. And I'm betting whoever that someone is, they aren't affiliated with the hedges."

"But that would create an imbalance in magic. The impact of that could be catastrophic. And not just for us." She saw the questioning look in Torie's eyes. "The ley lines aren't just there for us. They provide stability for many in the supernatural community. Some of our friends are tied directly into the health of those lines—"

A crash from downstairs caused the witches to jump from their chairs. Leo raised a sleepy head, alerted to a possible threat by Torie's body language.

"What was that?" Torie asked.

In answer, there came another series of crashes, the unmistakable howl of Elric in his full wolf form, followed by a full-throated roar from the werewolf.

Torie motioned to Leo, sending him a gentle push through their rapport. "You stay here. Stay by the fire, until I come back."

Reluctantly, the little dragon watched as the two witches raced from the bedroom and headed for the staircase. Together, they raced down the steps to be greeted by a large hallway console table crashing into the wall in front of them, splintering to pieces upon impact.

Jasmin shielded her face from flying debris and turned to face Torie. "Well, so much for not destroying the house again."

Tentatively, they made their way around the corner, the sounds of conflict and Elric's growls growing louder. They let out a collective gasp as they peered into the entry to see Elric circling Jax. The giant's eyes were gray and glassy, and blood dripped from an open wound on his forearm, courtesy of Elric's fangs. The wolf snarled a low warning as he looked for another opening to attack.

Other than the shredded arm, the giant didn't seem particularly interested in the werewolf, and instead fixed his eyes on Torie and Jasmin as they stepped into the room.

Following the giant's eyes, Elric roared his disapproval when he saw who Jax was staring at. The fur along the back of the wolf stood on end, his yellow eyes flared in anger.

"You up for this?" said Jasmin, her eyes taking on a green glow.

"Guess we'll find out," said Torie as she called to her magic.

Seeing the witches prepare to join the fray, Jax responded in a way no one expected. He lowered his head and dropped to his knees, arms at his side.

Seeing his opening, Elric's muscles bunched as he prepared to spring, razor-sharp fangs ready to close on the giant's head.

"Elric, no!" shouted Torie. She held her hand up, letting the werewolf know not to attack. He stood down, his eyes questioning as he slowly backed away, moving to crouch next to the witches.

The giant stared at them, his eerie, gray eyes both seeing and not seeing at the same time.

"What are you doing?" whispered Jasmin to her friend. "This might be our chance. Look at him, he's bleeding. That means he can be hurt."

Torie shook her head. "No. Something is off. Why isn't he attacking us? Why put himself in such a vulnerable position?" She looked at Elric. "What happened? Did he attack you?"

The wolf shifted, assuming his human form. "I heard something on the porch, and then I caught his scent. When I opened the door, he was standing there, and he just walked into the house, pushing past me."

"But did he attack you?" Torie asked again.

Elric thought and shook his head. "No. He wasn't aggressive. I just assumed he was here to try and harm you again."

Torie took a deep breath and slowly moved toward the giant. A wave of her hand let her friends know that she was alright, and not to make any sudden movements. When she was within reach of the giant, he turned his head slightly in her direction, acknowledging her presence. Stretching a hand out, Torie placed it lightly on Jax's shoulder. The giant didn't move as he continued to study her face.

Holding out her hand, Torie summoned a clean towel from the linen closet and gently applied it to the tear in Jax's forearm. She applied pressure and then nodded for Jasmin and Elric to join them. The giant's eyes wandered briefly over Elric before settling back on Torie.

"He isn't here to fight," Torie said.

"Then what does he want?" replied Jasmin.

"Why don't we ask him? We know he can speak, at least in a rudimentary way," Torie said.

Jasmin pursed her lips. "Maybe we can help with that."

She extended a hand, placing it on Jax's chest, and spoke.

"From the depths of silence, let your voice arise,
to speak your truth, and uncloud your eyes.
Let it find its voice, with strength new found,
So that its message may be heard, and its spirit unbound."

Warmth and magic flowed from her hand into the giant. Jax gasped, throwing his head back to face the ceiling. When he looked back at them, his gray eyes had lost their lifeless luster and were replaced with a silver light that stared intently at the witches.

"Thank you," he said in a voice that was deep, yet still hesitant. His tone was wavering and unsure. It was as if his voice was being forced to make sounds it had not made in years.

Torie removed the cloth from his arm, surprised to see

the wound was already beginning to heal. "Jax, can you understand us?"

He nodded in response, raising one had to his throat to massage his neck. "I can. I always could, but this body was not designed to speak. And trying to force it to was an exercise in frustration, to say the least."

Jasmin raised her eyebrows, surprised at the words coming from the giant. "Jax, why are you here?"

"To warn you. You're in greater danger than you could ever imagine." The giant looked at her with silver eyes shining. "And I'm not Jax. I'm Eliza."

Chapter Twenty-Five

Torie led the group into the large sitting area, the shock of the giant's words hanging in the air. "I see that your arm is healing, but is there anything you need?"

The giant's head shook slowly. "All that I need is to warn you." Looking down at its hands, the giant sighed. "And I don't know how much longer I have. This body was not meant to act as a vessel. I won't be able to maintain this for long."

"I don't even know where to start," said Jasmin, dropping into a chair opposite.

"How about we start with the truth," said Torie. "What did you do to Malena?"

The giant looked at her, and for the first time, Torie thought she could make out emotions in its eyes.

The creature called Eliza sighed. "I did what I had to. I placed a binding spell on her. One that was meant to partition her off from accessing her abilities until I could find a way to help her. And, if I couldn't help her, I needed to find a way to destroy her."

Jasmin saw red, her eyes blazing darkly. "Destroy her? You were her mother."

Eliza looked at her through a stranger's eyes, lowering her head. "And while it shames me to admit that, it is better than what could now potentially happen. And while yes, I was tasked with raising Malena, I am not her biological mother."

"If you're not her mother, who is?" asked Torie. "And what about Clive?"

Eliza sighed. "Clive was her biological father. He and I met shortly after her birth. We've spent the time since then trying to learn all we could about Malena. Who and what she is, and what she was meant to do." She took a deep breath, letting it out slowly. "Malena is what is known as a cambion. And before you ask, a cambion is the offspring of a human male and a succubus." She watched as the meaning of her words settled in.

"I've heard of such things," said Elric. "But I didn't believe they were actually possible."

"It shouldn't be possible," said Jasmin. "Despite what the legends claim."

"What am I missing here?" asked Torie. "I've a feeling I'm the only one who doesn't know what we are talking about."

"A succubus is a female demon who appears in the dreams of men to seduce them..." said Eliza. Her voice trailed off and she stared off into space, her mouth hanging slightly open.

Jasmin and Torie exchanged glances before Torie reached forward, waving her hand in front of the giant's face. "Hey, are you okay? Still with us?"

Slowly, after a few seconds of confusion, the giant came back into focus. "Forgive me. I am starting to drift. As I said, this body was not created to be inhabited by the presence of another. I can feel myself slipping away in it." She leaned forward, eyes widening. "That is why it is so imperative that you understand. I failed. You must succeed where I could not." Her voice was deep and raw, anguish poured from every part of the giant's being.

"What can we do?" asked Torie.

"You removed the sigil that bound her. It's too late to put it back. You need to find her and destroy her before she can join them," said Eliza.

"Join who?" asked Elric.

Torie could tell the conversation was making him more and more nervous as he paced the floor.

"Malena's birth was orchestrated by a monster that has its eyes on your little town of Singing Falls. The pairing of that succubus with Clive was not random. For reason we never knew, Clive was chosen to father her with that particular succubus. The creature that arranged it wanted the offspring in order to complete whatever hellish plans it has for Singing Falls."

Jasmin let out a sharp breath. "What kind of creature commands demons? Who is this being?"

The giant shook its head. "I don't know. But you've met it." Eliza's eyes focused on Torie.

The shock she felt was like a slap in the face for Torie.

"The shadow creature. The thing that grabbed me and imprisoned me in that bottle."

Eliza was nodding. "He's stronger here. That's why he was able to do that. He's found a new source of power to tap into."

The two witches exchanged looks.

"The ley lines," said Jasmin. "That would explain what

you were seeing, Torie. They must have appeared sick because he was there, actively tapping into their power."

Torie turned her attention to the giant. "If he is capable of doing that, what possible need does he have for Malena?"

"She is a living conduit. The succubus who gave birth to her was a variant. A form of demon that grew from a corruption of earth magic. One that existed outside of the dark realm where such creatures are normally found. The shadow beast you encountered has been trying to devise a way to get a foothold into this realm for ages. Now, by engineering the birth of a creature that will allow him to tap into what you term ley lines, he will no longer need agents. He can operate freely in this realm."

Torie's breathing had quickened, and her blood felt like ice. She looked over at Jasmin and could tell her friend had the same chilling thoughts.

"This creature," said Torie slowly, "Has it tried to breach the veil between worlds recently?"

"I believe so," said Eliza. "Clive was the expert on this monster, and he had tracked its activity to this area before he was killed. That is what brought me here. He said the two of you had thwarted the beast once before, when he sought to blind the fates that protected this realm."

Torie felt the air rush out of her, and the room spun lightly around her. She cradled her head in her hands. "Oh, my God." She looked at Jasmin. "That's what was behind the horrors that cost me Shawn."

"Why was Clive killed? And did Malena do that?" asked Jasmin.

"No," replied Eliza, "She did not. She was with me when that happened. The best I can figure is that he was killed by someone working with the shadow creature to keep Clive from talking to you."

Jasmin was nodding. "That would explain what he was doing on that plateau where the lunarwort grows. Somehow, he knew we would be up there."

"And your coven? Why did you bring them here from up north?" Torie asked.

"I needed a reason to join Clive down here. One that wouldn't trigger Malena. So, the pretense of setting up a new coven seemed perfect at the time. Plus, I had hopes that a hedge witch coven would be able to assist in defeating this monster. But now...all I've done is put everyone in danger. Gotten Michael and Seraph killed. Doomed this body..." Her voice was filled with remorse as her eyes drifted to the giant's hands. "Jax was created to be my bodyguard. A powerful sentinel meant only to protect, no matter the cost. But he wasn't able to stop the shadow creature. It is tethered to Malena in this realm, and when she entered my prayer room, it was able to gain access long enough to launch an attack on me. When I realized I wasn't going to survive, I leapt into this body, leaving mine just as they burned me. But now..." Again, she glanced at the massive trembling hands.

Torie sensed that whatever was happening to the giant, they didn't have much time to get more information. She breathed out, sending a comforting plume of magic to suffuse the giant, to give Eliza strength.

The giant shuddered and offered a slight smile. "Thank you. That feels good." She basked in the warmth of Torie's magic before letting out a sigh.

"Eliza, I have to ask. Are you a hex witch?" Jasmin questioned.

The giant seemed startled. "Heavens no. Whatever gave you that idea?"

"Well, both Michael and Seraph said you were able to do a lot of magic that hedge witches could not. Even Malena said you were something more," said Torie.

"And there's the fact that you were able to waltz in here through our wards. Wards that seemed to stop that shadow creature," added Jasmin.

Eliza nodded. "I see. That would be because this body was created by an old associates of Clive. And I wore a number of baubles and charms gifted to me by him that allowed me to tap into his powers when I needed. Well, up until the time he was killed that is. But you're right. Hex magic is the only thing that so far confounds the beast. But with his living conduit now unlocked, who knows if that will still be the case."

Jasmin and Torie exchanged frowns, unsure how to proceed with the conversation.

Eliza sighed again. "Everything that has happened up until this point was designed to get you involved. Enacted by Malena. All she wanted was to get you to free her. Only hex magic could break the lock. Of course, little does she realize that in bringing you two into the fight, she has unwittingly given me what I needed as well. And that is to make you understand the urgency of what you are dealing with."

Something she said sparked a thought for Torie. "Eliza, you just said that only hex magic could break the lock binding Malena. That would imply that it was created by hex magic. But you said you aren't a hex witch."

The giant offered a lazy smile. "You do realize the two of you aren't the only hex witches in existence, right?" Eliza's silver eyes widened at the look on their faces. "Oh my. You didn't know. There are many covens out there in the world. Granted, not all of them are sitting in a supernatural haven the way you two are, but they're out there. Very secretive and hard to find. But Clive was familiar with more than a couple of hex witches. It was their coven that..." Again she paused, her voice drifting away. "Wait...what were we talking about?"

Torie leaned forward; her hands closed tightly together. "Eliza, concentrate. You were just telling us about the hex witch coven. You mentioned Clive's associate. Where is she?"

The giant's head tilted to one side. The eyes strayed, taking in the room. "What? Clive...yes...he was so good to me. And he so wanted to help Malena. But then...no...it's all so confusing. Everything is becoming gray."

Torie reached out, physically and mystically, using her magic to once again wash over the giant, flooding Eliza with warmth and calm. "Eliza, please...hang on just a bit more and finish telling us what we need to know so we can help you. So we can help Malena."

Eliza's eyes seemed to draw into focus in that moment as she studied the two witches. "I am sorry. I don't think I remember what we were talking about. It feels like there is something...something inside my head. It's eating away my memories..."

The giant's voice was fragmenting. Losing the softness and the tone of Eliza as the harshness of Jax worked its way back in.

The giant's head shook from side to side as Eliza momentarily came back, throwing the witches a pleading look. "This body is far too powerful to fall into dark and malevolent hands. Jax has served me so well. But he's gone now. He was gone the moment my body was destroyed. I am begging you, don't let him be used by...them." Silver eyes met Jasmin and Torie's as tears rolled down the giant's cheek.

Torie nodded, blinking rapidly to fight back her own sorrows at what had to be done.

The giant turned to face the door. Eliza offered them a weak smile. "I need to see the stars and all the beauty that mother nature grants us one last time."

They followed her outside to the patch of manicured lawn encircled by the driveway. The giant stood there, face to the sky, a single tear visible to the witches who stood to either side.

Together, Torie and Jasmin raised their hands, syncing their magic and their voices as they called the power of the hex.

> *"Under the power of the moon and the stars above,*
> *we release this soul with grace and love.*
> *Let it wander free to soar and find its way,*
> *to a peaceful place where it may stay.*
> *We bid farewell to the shell of this one,*
> *its time has passed, its purpose done.*
> *May you both find peace and rest,*
> *in a world beyond that is truly blessed."*

Magic flowed around and through the giant. Silver vapors that danced and entwined, circling until they slowly closed in, entering the creature that sheltered the soul of Eliza. Power flared as the giant began to break apart like mist dissolving under sunlight, becoming part of nature itself.

As the giant melted away, Eliza's voice floated through the air one last time. "Beware the Umbrali, my sisters..."

The words were faint and broken by the slight breeze that blew across the yard, carrying the last vestiges of Eliza away.

Once she was gone, Torie took Jasmin's hand, weeping silently, as they made their way back into the house.

Chapter Twenty-Six

The inside of the bakery smelled of fresh baked bread, sweet jams, toasted cinnamon and the pure magical elixir that was fresh brewed coffee. Fionna joined Jasmin and Torie at one of the tables. It was late afternoon, and the shop was unusually quiet.

"So where are we with everything?" Fionna asked.

Torie sighed, taking a slow sip of coffee. "Well, the way I see it we have two options. The first is we wait and see what happens. We know that Malena is out there, in service to some otherworldly beast. But neither of them has made a move. It could be that this creature has what it needs and has moved on. So now we wait for them to make the next move."

Fionna frowned, casting a glance Jasmin's way. "Yeah, that doesn't sound like a solid plan to me."

Jasmin smiled, stretching her arms languidly overhead. "Or, we track down this monster and put an end to it before it can kill one of us or someone we care about."

Fionna gave a sharp nod and a wink at Jasmin.

"Between those two, you know which one I'm leaning towards."

Torie didn't say anything, just continued to sip her coffee. She thought back to when they used their power to dissolve the sentinel who had once protected Eliza and had ended up becoming her living tomb. And even though it had been a kindness, there was a sadness in the act that she feared would haunt her until the day she died.

"This feels like an iceberg. Like, we're only seeing the top of it. The rest, the part that will do the most damage, is buried deep, waiting for us to stumble into it," she said.

Both women remained silent, and then Fionna piped up. "Then we learn more. Develop a detailed analysis of the threat. Come up with the best way to neutralize it."

Jasmin was nodding. "Yes. It's not like we don't have resources at our disposal. From the sound of things, it isn't just Singing Falls that is in danger now. And we know from our past encounter with these demons, for lack of a better word, that they have a darker vision in mind than we can probably imagine." She reached over and gave Torie's hand a squeeze. "This is not something we can just be reactive to."

Torie smiled lazily. "I know. And that's why I asked Max to investigate the hedge witch coven a little deeper. We need to get to the original coven up north. Surely one member here has had ties to the first coven. I just have the feeling that that's where we will find answers to questions we haven't yet thought of."

Jasmin regarded her friend, her lips pressed tightly together. "It's more than that, isn't it? You're thinking about Malena."

Torie exhaled sharply and sat her cup down. "I just

can't help but think there is an innocent girl in there, being used by forces she can't possibly comprehend."

Jasmin stared at her friend, swallowing hard before continuing. "She's not Shawn, Torie."

The truth of her words stung, and Torie didn't have an answer.

Fionna huffed. "Don't forget, she wasn't under anyone's control when she poisoned me and then pretended like nothing happened. And who knows what really happened to Eliza in that prayer room. Everything that girl has done has shown just how black her heart can be. I think you can only truly corrupt something that's already a bit twisted."

"Torie, she's a cambion," Jasmin added. "The more I've read up on those, the more I'm inclined to agree with Fionna on this. She's half demon, so that makes her an easy target for the shadows to corrupt. And if, as Eliza said, she was created with the sole purpose of aiding this creature, then we really only have one choice."

Torie didn't answer. She knew they were right. But she also knew that if there was even a chance to save that girl, she was going to try it. "You're right. But she's also half human. Still, if it comes down to it, I won't hesitate to do what's needed to save this community, and anyone else."

"Whatever happens, we face it together," Jasmin replied, then turned to Fionna. "All of us."

"So many questions," Torie said. "I still don't understand what Eliza meant by 'Umbrali'. For those to be her final words, they have to be key to what's going on."

"I've been looking into that," said Jasmin. "It's from the Latin word umbral, which means shadow or obscurity. It's also Spanish and Portuguese for threshold."

"So, maybe it's a portal to someplace dark. You've dealt with those before, right?" said Fionna.

"Maybe," said Torie, thinking hard. Her eyes widened as she looked at her friends. "Or maybe, in this case, it's a person. Or a group of people. A cabal of some sort."

"That would make sense," said Jasmin. "And it would be in keeping with the context in which Eliza told us to beware."

"So much of this comes back to unanswered questions about Eliza and her coven," said Jasmin.

"And other hex witches operating out there. Someone had to have been working very closely with Eliza and Clive to cast the spells they had. What if that person is now in danger as well?" asked Torie. "Maybe that's where we should start. There should be a spell we can come up with that will locate another hex witch, right?"

"Actually, you can save your magic."

Their heads turned just as Max and Elric were walking up.

Max dropped a manilla envelope onto the coffee table. "We went back to the mansion just to do some follow up questioning. That place has been cleaned out."

"The stench of blood and cleaning agents is all over the place," added Elric.

Jasmin's hands flew to her mouth as she gasped. "Those poor people. Maybe we can—"

Max cut her off. "I don't know what happened there and probably don't want to know. But in scouring the place we did find this left behind. It was hidden in the emptied-out library."

Torie opened the envelope to find an old, grainy, black and white photograph of a younger Eliza and another woman they didn't recognize. "This looks like Eliza, but who is she with?"

Elric took a deep breath. "Take a look at the back."

Torie turned the picture over and gasped at the inscription. "Eliza Fairchild and Rowena Blackwood. But—" she hesitated, a deep frown marring her face, "—this picture is dated...1898. How is that possible?" She handed the picture to Jasmin and Fionna to study. "That would mean she is over one hundred and twenty-five years old. If that's true, what was she?"

"Only one way to find out. We did some digging through—let's just say *unofficial* channels—and we found out that Rowena Blackwood is still alive and kicking as well."

"No way," said Jasmin in awe.

Elric was nodding. "Last known address is a tiny little hamlet just outside of...Salem, Massachusetts."

Torie nodded, her eyes lighting up. "Well. Looks like we need to take a little road trip."

Jasmin smiled. "You know, I always did want to visit Salem. See what all the fuss was about."

Fionna frowned. "Why would you want to go there? They executed witches. Maybe they still do up there."

Emerald light sparked from Jasmin's eyes. "I'd like to see them try."

Torie felt her heart flutter, but her resolve stiffened. "Well then. It looks like we're off to speak with Rowena Blackwood and get some answers as to what is really going on around here."

It was a single, declarative statement. But it was one she knew was about to lead her and her friends into a world more dangerous and darker than any they had yet faced.

Chapter Twenty-Seven

From the outside, the house looked like any other modern home. It was an imposing two-story structure with a sloping roof and large picture windows that looked out onto a neatly manicured lawn. There were no warning signs about security systems, no cameras, no doorbells that allowed for two-way communication with anyone who might approach. The front door was a wood veneer over reinforced steel, with a small peephole and a keypad lock that required a passcode to open. No lights could be seen through the blacked-out windows that flanked the entry.

Inside the house, there was a single, long hallway leading from the door. There were no windows along it to let in natural light. The only sources of illumination were tall torches along the stone walls topped with flickering flames that sent shadows dancing across the high ceiling. At the end of the hallway was a single door.

Inside was a large chamber. A massive, round table carved from a single piece of dark, polished wood dominated the room. It was surrounded by high-backed chairs, and at each seat was a small, glowing orb that cast an eerie blue light into the otherwise darkened space. Each orb pulsed and swirled with energy before dimming respectfully as a single, shadowy figure, cloaked in a mist of gray vapors stood.

"Rest easy my friends. We needn't be worried." His voice dripped with malice as it crawled forth.

"But they are aware of us now," said another from the far side of the table.

"Yes. They are. But there is little they can do. We have the conduit now. Soon, everything we have worked so hard for will come to fruition." The shadow looked around the table. "And remember, unlike before, we have been able to extract bits of their magic this time. Thanks to the conduit, we know how their spells work. We now understand the need for intent behind what they conjure. We were able to take their own enchanted charm and turn it into a working trap that held one of them prisoner. And thanks to them, we now have the full power of the Alchemicon unlocked. We have never been more prepared."

Another voice, like frost cracking on a window, rose from the assemblage. "And if they find Rowena?"

The shadow's voice rolled forth again. "She will most likely kill them. And if she does not, it won't matter. We have everything we need. We have survived their kind before, and we will survive these. The Convergence comes soon, and when it does, the ley lines will be ours to command. And once that happens, the witches will be as dust before us. The time of the hex has passed. Long live the Umbrali."

vinci-books.com/hexfactor

The race against time has begun—who will survive the magic's grip?

As a dark power rises in Singing Falls, only Torie holds the key to stopping it. But at what price will victory come?

Turn the page for a free preview…

That Hex Factor: Chapter One

Torie bolted upright in bed, her hand on her throat, a scream locked in her chest. She was covered in sweat, the pounding of her heart so loud in her ears that she was certain it could be heard throughout the house.

Squeezing her eyes shut, she slammed a fist into the mattress, telling herself it wasn't real, that it was just a dream. No matter how real it felt at the time, it was only a dream.

Of course, it didn't help that it was the same one she had experienced constantly over the last few nights.

It started off pleasant enough, with her walking the grounds of a beautiful Federal-style house, with lovely gardens overlooking a large pond. But without fail, as she walked, everything around her would begin to morph into something unrecognizable. The white siding of the house would melt and puddle like ice cream sliding down a cone on a sunny day. The flowers in the garden wilted, their petals dropping to become pock marks on the browning grass.

That's when she would turn and run, fear telling her not to look back, but to keep driving her legs forward to get away from what was to come. Only she couldn't run. The ground beneath her became soft and soggy, pulling her in to her knees. She would reach upward to the heavens, screaming for someone to pull her free, only to have the earth reach up with dark tentacles made of sticky tar and wrap themselves around her, pulling her backwards and deeper into the ground.

She would open her mouth to scream, only to have it fill with dirt as she was swallowed whole. She would awaken, gulping air and clutching at her chest, lost in the haze of her nightmare.

In the darkness of the room, she felt a comforting, warm buzzing in her lap. The iridescent display of lights playing along Leo's scales helped to ground her. The soft vibration passing through his body, and the soft, loving emerald glow of his eyes told Torie she is safe in this space.

Letting out a deep breath, she stroked Leo's back, luxuriating in the tranquility he radiated.

"My little therapy dragon," she said quietly into the darkness. Reaching to her side, she felt the empty space where Elric had been. She smiled down at Leo. "Oh well, I guess somebody got tired of being awakened by my night terrors." She leaned forward, snuggling her face against the dragon's snout. "But not you. Not mama's little baby."

Once he was content everything was alright, Leo hopped off the bed and made his way back to the little cushion he had adopted as his bed, and curled back up, tiny wisps of smoke exiting his nostrils as he fell almost immediately back into a deep sleep.

Torie tossed about, flipping her pillow to the cooler side,

and finally drifted off for a bit, knowing that dawn was only hours away.

Light pouring in through the windows came all too swiftly, and she dragged herself from the bed, threw on a robe, and followed her nose to the kitchen. The smell of freshly brewed coffee, bacon, eggs, and the sweet scent of cinnamon and maple that hinted at French toast all but made her salivate.

"Good morning," she said to Elric, as she made her way to the doors to let Leo out. She left it open for him to return once he was done with his business and moved to stand next to Elric at the stove, stretching onto her tip-toes to give him a quick kiss. "Did I wake you up last night?"

The big wolf shook his head while flipping a piece of toast. "Not at all. I couldn't sleep so I went for a run. Full moon is drawing close."

Torie nodded. She was usually pretty good about keeping up with the cycles of the moon, knowing how it could affect werewolves, but lately she was more wrapped up in what was going on in her own mind.

"Why do you ask?" Elric said. "More of those dreams?"

She nodded, moving over to the island where she grabbed a piece of bacon to crunch on. "It's so weird. It's the same one. The details never change."

Elric turned off the range and spun around to face her, holding a plate of French toast in one hand and a tray of eggs in the other. He made his way to the island just as the cupboards opened and a couple of plates flew from them to settle gracefully in front of Torie.

"There's fresh squeezed orange juice in the fridge," he

said, nodding at the gleaming silver Sub-Zero that hulked along one wall.

Torie grabbed the OJ and returned, staring at all the food. "Is someone coming over I don't know about? You made enough for a family get together." She saw him arch a single eyebrow and couldn't help but break into a smile. "Or a witch, a hungry werewolf and a bottomless pit masquerading as a baby dragon."

Elric laughed, taking a seat beside her as they both began loading their plates. The wolf smiled, leaning over and giving a few slabs of bacon to a patiently waiting Leo, before addressing Torie. "You know, I really think you need to talk to someone about these nightmares. I don't know who...but isn't there some kind of hotline or therapist you can reach out to?"

Torie gave him a weak grin and shook her head. "No, not quite. You're the closest thing I have to that. Well, and Jasmin of course. And she is already buried in research trying to figure out what they mean."

The mention of her best friend, and fellow witch, made her briefly wonder where Jasmin was. It wasn't like her not to show up for breakfast, especially after Torie had let her know French toast was on the menu.

Elric cleared his throat. "I mean, it's pretty obvious what's going on."

Torie raised her eyebrows and set down her cup of juice. "Oh? Do tell."

He swallowed a mouthful of golden toast, dabbing at a drop of maple syrup on his lips. "Torie, you were kidnapped and locked in a bottle, sealed away from everything. You almost died, my dear. It doesn't take a psychoanalyst to connect the dots. In your dreams, the earth is swallowing you whole, trapping you. You are reliving your trauma."

Torie smiled, giving her boyfriend her complete attention. "Is that your professional opinion?"

"I'm a wolf. In my opinion, the simplest explanation is usually the right one."

Torie sighed, pushing the plate in front of her away. "I wish it were that simple. But this feels so different. It's so real. And while it's hard to explain, it feels like it is getting more real each night." She shook her head and took her plate with leftovers on it and sat it on the floor in front of Leo. She held up one finger in admonishment. "And no charring the food. You've burned up enough of my plates doing that."

The little dragon murmured something deep from his chest as he buried his face happily in the plate.

"I think he just talked back to you," said Elric.

Torie laughed. "It's like he's hitting his terrible-twos or something." Despite his sometimes-sassy demeanor, she couldn't help but be filled with love every time she looked at Leo.

"You know, he's growing fast," said Elric. His tone was more leading than just making a statement.

"I know. But he's still just a little thing."

"Yes, but he's a dragon. Who knows how long he'll be little?"

She knew what he was saying. It wasn't anything she hadn't heard from Jasmin before. And truthfully it had occurred to her as well. But she pushed such thoughts to the back of her mind.

"I don't care how big he gets. He's my family now."

Elric smiled, looking from Torie to the dragon that was literally licking his plate clean. "That's true. He's saved you a couple of times now. I guess he's not going anywhere." He stood up and began clearing the island and loading the dishwasher.

"You know, the house will do that for you," Torie said.

He shrugged. "I know. But I kind of like doing it myself. When the house does it, there's something creepy about it."

Torie folded her arms. "Are you saying my magic creeps you out?"

Elric gave her one of his lopsided grins and wrapped his arms around her. "Your magic is the farthest thing from creepy. I love it when you hex me." Torie threw her head back in laughter. "But when I get out of the shower and there's a towel floating in the air waiting for me? Creepy."

"Okay, I'll give you that," said Torie. "But you'll get used to it."

Elric let out a playful groan. "That's what I'm afraid of." He pulled away and resumed his cleaning. "So, what's on tap for today?"

"I'm meeting Jasmin at the bakery this morning. We are going to go over everything we've been able to learn about Rowena Blackwood, which isn't much at all, and what we've learned about the supernatural community in Salem, before we head up there."

Elric didn't say anything, but Torie could see the tension creep into his frame. The muscles in his back strained at the tee shirt he wore as he increased the speed with which he scrubbed the range top.

"We have to do this, Elric."

He sighed, his head dropping. "I know. Really, I do. But that doesn't mean I have to like it. And I'd feel better if I were by your side when you go."

"And I appreciate that. Truth be told I'd probably feel a lot better knowing you were with me. But we agreed it was better that you stayed here."

He half turned his head in her direction. "Did we though?"

She smiled. "Well, we agreed in principal. With everything happening, I know Max will be more comfortable with you here to back him up. It feels like we are being hit on multiple fronts here. He trusts you, and right now he needs you at his side."

Elric didn't say anything, only nodding as he continued his assault on the Viking range. Torie was right of course. In a town that was comprised of a lot of supernatural creatures, the sheriff would need all the help he could get if something dark was afoot.

And there was something very dark in the works.

"Just...promise you'll be careful. You don't know who or what this Rowena person is. Don't take any chances."

"No chances. I promise." She loved the way he longed to protect her. In the beginning of their relationship, she had been somewhat taken aback, thinking that he didn't believe she was capable of taking care of herself. That she needed a man to always protect her. But now, she realized that his actions weren't driven from his own desire to control her, or by any outdated machismo ideals.

No. He loved her. Pure and simple. And he would do anything in the world to keep her safe. And there was a truth and a warmth in that purity that she had never known before.

"I'm going for a run," Elric said. He gave the stove one last glance before disposing of the wipe in the trash.

Torie nodded. "Are you okay?"

He gave her a genuine smile. "I am. Promise. I just have a lot of excess energy this close to a full moon. Need to burn a little more."

"Okay. Now it's my turn to tell you to be careful out

there." She gave him a peck on the lips as he headed for the back door. "I'll see you later this evening and let you know what we come up with."

"Sounds good," he said, then disappeared out the door and across the patio.

Torie watched as he disappeared, leaping over the iron fence and dropping out of view.

She took a deep breath and steeled herself for what was to come. With a sigh, she made her way back to the bedroom. She had just enough time for a shower before meeting Jasmin and Fionna at the bakery the three of them had purchased. Instinctively, she reached out with her mind, feeling for the protective wards around the house, strengthening them with a whisper. The memory of her nightmare clawed its way into her mind once again, and she shivered.

Something was coming. She could feel it deep inside. And no matter how much magic she poured into the wards around her, she wasn't certain she would be able to keep it out.

That Hex Factor: Chapter Two

As Torie pushed open the door to the Brew Cup Bakery, the charming, tinkling melody of the door chime set the tone for a cozy and welcoming atmosphere. Fionna had truly outdone herself on the decor, and both Torie and Jasmin couldn't have been prouder of her choices.

The bakery was bathed in warm, amber light emanating from antique brass fixtures hanging from the ceiling. The walls were adorned with vintage, floral-patterned wallpaper and lined with wooden shelves housing an assortment of antique pans and kitchenware from years gone by.

The aroma of freshly baked goods enveloped Torie, a tantalizing blend of buttery croissants, rich chocolate, and the faintest hint of cinnamon and fresh berries. Even though she had just eaten, the scent was intoxicating and stirred her hunger. As she inhaled deeply, she could almost taste the sugary sweetness of the raspberry-filled Danishes and the flaky, buttery layers of the golden-brown Palmiers.

It was early morning, but the place was already quite busy. A soft jazz tune played in the background, melding with the pleasant hum of conversation from the humans gathered around the mismatched antique tables, sipping on steaming mugs of coffee and tea. The gentle clinking of porcelain and silverware, coupled with the sound of laughter, created a welcoming atmosphere of comfort and belonging.

However, it was the subtle details Fionna had added that truly made Brew Cup Bakery a haven for supernaturals. Upon closer inspection, the intricate wallpaper pattern revealed tiny crescent moons and stars hidden amidst the flowers—a symbol of the safe space this bakery provided. An ethereal glow, perceptible only to supernatural beings, emanated from a beautifully crafted stained-glass window featuring a waning moon and an array of mythical creatures dancing in the night sky.

A faint, but noticeable, scent of sage and lavender lingered in the air, the remnants of a protection spell woven by Torie and Jasmin that was meant to safeguard any supernaturals who sought refuge within the bakery's walls. The spell, undetectable to humans, provided a sense of security and peace for the magical patrons.

Behind the glass display case, Fionna stood with Tara, one of her new employees. She whispered conspiratorially to the young girl, who giggled in response. Fionna looked up to Torie as she entered, giving her a nod and an inviting smile. She was dressed in jeans and a sleeveless tee shirt that showed off her toned arms. The only jewelry, other than her wedding band, was a silver pendant with an intricate tree of life design resting on her chest.

"Well, hey there," she said, her voice warm and soothing, like a cup of hot cocoa on a cold winter's night. "Grab our seats. I'll be over in a second."

As Torie stepped farther into the enchanting bakery, she

couldn't help but feel a sense of belonging wash over her. Here, she was not just another customer. She was not just an owner. She was part of a secret world where the magical and the mundane intertwined; a harmonious symphony that celebrated the extraordinary.

Torie made her way to the enormous fireplace dominating the back of the cafe. There was a table with three high-backed leather chairs that sat facing the hearth.

Their chairs.

Despite the fact that the cafe had no reservation system in place, no matter how busy it was, these seats were always open. It was as if everyone just knew who that space belonged to.

Torie approached the chairs and was happy to see Jasmin already seated, discreet jewelry sparkling against her yellow sundress, her afro a glorious halo of a cloud.

"There you are," said Torie. "I missed you at breakfast this morning."

"Oh. Was it French toast?" Just the tiniest pang of longing in her voice.

Torie nodded. "And the extra-crispy bacon."

Jasmin shook her head and let out a sigh. "Girl, you know I can't be eating like that anymore. I'm at a point where all that salt is not good for me. And all that sugar goes right to my hips and stays there." She gave Torie a playful up and down look. "But it seems like having a wolf full time in residence is agreeing with you. How are you staying so fit?"

Torie rolled her eyes. "It's because that man loves to work out. And he makes me do it with him most of the time."

Jasmin's eyes narrowed and her brows danced comically. "Oh, I bet he does."

Torie laughed and playfully slapped at her friend's arm just as Fionna approached with a tray laden with two French presses and a tray of fresh baked scones.

"What's so funny?" she asked.

"Just laughing at how good Elric has been for Torie," said Jasmin. "She's been getting her workouts in."

Fionna joined in the laughter. "You two are great together. Isn't it about time you make it official?"

Torie rolled her eyes again, waving Fionna off. Then she noticed Jasmin wasn't saying anything, and instead was pouring herself a cup of coffee.

"Jas – why did you suddenly go radio silent?" Torie said, squinting at her friend.

Jasmin looked at her, eyes wide. "What? Nothing. Unlike some people, I haven't eaten all morning and have been looking forward to diving into these scones. Is that alright?" She returned to fixing her coffee and making a point of shoveling a big bite of her scone into her mouth.

"Uh-huh," said Torie, reaching for a cup while side-eyeing her friend.

Fionna dropped into the third chair and reached for a scone. "Well, did you two decide what you're going to do about the whole Salem thing? Are you waiting it out or paying that Rowena person a visit?"

Torie nervously gnawed on her bottom lip; her eyes wide as she contemplated. "We have to go to her," she said hesitantly.

Jasmin nodded, her expression solemn and serious. "Yes. We've tried a variety of revelation spells as well as communication and location ones. All to no avail. So, all that's left is an in-person visit."

Fionna nodded, taking a small nibble of her scone. "When are you leaving?"

"Tomorrow," said Jasmin. "And there's still plenty of seats left on the plane if you want to join us."

They had asked Fionna before and knew her answer had most likely not changed.

Fionna looked down, her leg bouncing with anxious energy. "You guys know I have your back no matter what, right? But shifters and planes don't mix. Especially not me. I mean, we're meant to be close to the ground, not soaring so far above it. Just the thought of being so far removed from the earth...it's just not natural. I'm breaking out in a cold sweat just thinking about it."

Torie reached out, placing a protective hand on her friend's knee. "You don't have to explain yourself. Ever. We wouldn't have asked a second time, but just wanted to make sure you hadn't changed your mind."

Fionna smiled and covered Torie's hand with her own.

"Well, I guess the good thing is, someone will be here to keep this place running. You really have done amazing things here," said Jasmin.

"Agreed," added Torie. "It's more than I could have ever imagined."

Fionna beamed with pride. "Well, now all we have to do is keep it from being destroyed by malignant forces or more bodies showing up here."

Jasmin cleared her throat. "And that's why we are going to Salem. Whatever Eliza's old coven may know could help us to figure out what's going on here. Before it's too late."

Torie shuddered at her friend's words.

Jasmin gave her a concerned look. "What is it?"

Torie sighed, sipping her coffee. "More bad dreams. Can't seem to shake them."

"Did you try the herbal tea I gave you?" asked Jasmin.

She nodded, letting out another sigh. "I did. Didn't help.

All it made me do was wake up from my nightmares needing to go to the bathroom really bad."

Fionna swallowed a bite of scone. "It's probably because you were stuck in that bottle. You're just reliving that." She stopped mid-chew as Torie gave her a look. "What?"

Torie was shaking her head. "Must be a shifter thing."

"Huh?" said Fionna, her confusion not interfering with her enjoyment of the scone.

"Never mind," said Torie. "Let's just say you aren't the first to tell me that." Torie frowned as she watched Fionna finish off the scone and reach for another. "Looks like Jasmin wasn't the only one who didn't eat this morning."

Fionna stopped chewing and stared at the pastry in her hand. "Wow. I didn't even realize I had grabbed another one. I think that's like the tenth thing I've eaten today. I can't seem to stop." She laughed politely and placed the scone on her napkin, sitting it back on the tray.

"Hey, if I were blessed with your metabolism, I'd eat like that too," said Jasmin.

Fionna shifted her weight in her seat, looking around the cafe. "Well, it's getting a bit busier. I need to go help the runner getting orders out. You'll give me a call before you board the plane, yes?"

"Of course," said Torie, standing up. "We'll let you know when we land as well."

They said their goodbyes with a quick embrace and watched as Fionna scooted off to disappear behind the glass counter and through the swinging metal doors that led to the bakery's kitchen.

"Did she seem okay to you?" Jasmin asked.

"I was just about to ask you the same thing."

They gathered their dishes and took them to the receptacle, scraping them into the bin and placing the tray and plate back on top before heading out into the sunlight.

Torie basked in the brightness of the day, tilting her head back to bathe in the golden rays. "How can everything be so beautiful on the outside, and so festering on the inside?" She looked down Main Street, watching the bustling foot traffic as people wandered in and out of the shops that lined the busy street. "Wow. It's busy everywhere today. Are there sales or something we don't know about?"

"Well, I did hear that the hardware store is having a buy two lightbulbs, get the third for free sale," said Jasmin.

Torie smiled. "We're lucky to live here, you know that."

Jasmin hooked her arm in Torie's as they headed down the street. "And that's why we are going to make sure nothing happens to Singing Falls."

They made their way a half-block down the street, heading for their cars. As they passed the tea shop, a man barreled into them as he rushed out the door.

"Oh, excuse me," said Torie instinctively, latching onto Jasmin's arm for support in order to keep from toppling over.

"What?" said the man, adjusting a set of eyeglasses and looking around nervously. "Yes, you need to be excused. You're in my way."

Jasmin narrowed her eyes. "Hey, just a minute. You ran into us. Almost knocked us down."

The man shuffled in place, his eyes darting around nervously. "Of course. You're right. Entirely my fault. I...I don't know why I was in such a hurry."

Torie opened her mouth to say that it was alright, but before she could, the man's face changed. It was quick, and she barely noticed it, but his face narrowed, his nose elongated briefly, and his two front teeth became very pronounced. He opened his mouth and barked a high-pitched squeal at the women, causing them both to jump back.

Then, just as quickly as it happened, his face was back to normal. Shock and embarrassment flooded his features as a hand shot to his mouth. His eyes were wide in disbelief and all he could do was shake his head as he turned and rushed away from the witches.

"What in the world was that about?" asked Jasmin.

Torie narrowed her eyes, watching as the man receded from them. "No idea. But the sooner we find this Rowena woman and find out what she knows, the better I'll feel about things."

That Hex Factor: Chapter Three

Espresso.

That was what the morning called for. Torie was up at first light, waiting for the fancy, wall-unit coffee maker that no one in the house used, to finally chug out a tiny cup of condensed caffeine. It was just enough to shake off her residual drowsiness after yet another sleepless night.

Again, she had awakened to an empty bed, with only a concerned Leo to snuggle up to. Just as she drained the last drop of non-magical elixir from the cup, Elric walked in through the back doors, breathing heavily and soaked in sweat.

"Good morning," he said. "I went for another run. Couldn't sleep."

"Oh, okay. Well, are you still able to run me and Jasmin to the airport this morning?"

Elric looked at his watch, eyes wide. "Give me fifteen minutes to shower and change." He rushed off, and Torie could hear him loping up the stairs two at a time.

She shook her head and texted Jasmin, letting her know

they would swing by her house in thirty minutes to head to the airport.

Twenty minutes later, she was sitting in the living room, her travel bag next to her, tapping her foot as she waited for Elric. Finally, she went upstairs to find the wolf standing before the full-length mirror, running a comb through his hair, his eyes fixated on his reflection.

"Elric? What's going on? Are you coming down?"

The wolf looked at her absentmindedly. "Oh yeah...sorry." He started to follow her out of the bedroom, but she stopped him, looking down. He followed her gaze then grinned sheepishly as he realized he was only wearing a pair of boxers. "Oh! Sorry. I guess not sleeping is having an effect on me as well."

Grabbing his pants off the chair, along with a button-up shirt, he began pulling on his clothes while making his way towards the stairs.

"You sure you're okay?" Torie asked as they climbed into the car.

"Of course," he replied, climbing behind the wheel. "The moon phase will pass soon, and things will be back to normal. At least for another month."

They drove down the private road to the next driveway where Jasmin was waiting. Elric got out and loaded her suitcase in, squeezing it next to Torie's.

In minutes they were on their way, the big SUV easing out onto the winding mountainside roads that would take them to the regional airport nearly an hour away.

"Do you have everything we will need?" Torie asked, looking over her shoulder to her best friend.

"I think so. We've had no luck finding Rowena from here, but I'm hoping that if we're in the same town as she is, we should be able to find her with a divination spell. All we need to buy is a map of the area once we are there, and then we can use the divining crystals. I have to try and get a fix on her."

"And if that doesn't work?" Torie asked.

Jasmin's voice dropped. "Well, in that case, I have another, more direct method that might work."

Elric's eyes flitted to the rearview mirror briefly before settling back on the road. "I don't like the sound of that."

"Look, we don't have any idea what this Rowena woman is. We don't know for sure that we'll be able to locate her with magic, even if we are in her immediate vicinity. So, if we can't find her, then the next best thing..."

"Is to make her come to us," said Torie, finishing Jasmin's thought.

"Yeah, that really doesn't sound like a good plan. Maybe I should come with you. I can just run back and grab a couple of shirts. Or we could just drive up there—" He started pulling the SUV off the road to swing back around.

"No!" said both Torie and Jasmin in unison.

The car lurched as Elric jerked the wheel before steadying it back on the road.

"I mean, thank you," said Torie, "But we are going to be fine. We'll be gone for a day. Two at the most. Plus, you're really needed here. Something just feels off lately. I'd feel better knowing you're here watching Max's back."

"Plus, don't forget Leo," said Jasmin, giving Torie a quick glance.

"That's right," Torie said. "Who would look after him? You were looking forward to having some alone time with him, remember? I left his feeding schedule on the refrigerator door. No in between meal snacking, okay?"

Elric was focused on the road ahead, his brow furrowed. He must have sensed her staring at him because he gave her a quick glance and a smile. "What? Oh, yeah right. No, don't worry. The little guy's in good hands."

Torie frowned but went back to watching the foliage race by. In no time, Elric was easing the car to a stop in front of the North-Northwest airline terminal. Outside, they hurried to the back and started hauling out their bags. The noise of departing jets, blaring horns and loud voices put Torie a bit on edge, but she took the time to wrap her arms around Elric and promised to call him as soon as they landed. He gave her a quick kiss, and nervously shook hands with Jasmin, before pulling her in for a hug.

"Please take care of her," he whispered into her ear.

She gave him a reassuring squeeze on the shoulder, and they parted. Torie looked over her shoulder and waved as they pushed their way through the revolving door and into the crowded airport. Taking one look at the long check-in line and the even longer security line, she groaned.

"And now the fun part," she said to Jasmin.

Forty-five minutes later, they were sitting at their gate, waiting for boarding to start. Torie sipped on a water and Jasmin snacked on a bag of chips they had picked up at one of the seemingly endless shops lining the halls to all gates.

"I can't believe they have the nerve to charge these prices," Jasmin said. "This bag was more air than chips."

"We should have just tried a teleportation spell to get there," said Torie.

"I told you about that. It's one thing when we did it around here, moving from one place to another around Singing Falls. But over such a great distance? With no ley lines to guide us and make paths? It would have been too dangerous. We could have gotten lost and ended up who knows where."

Torie sighed, sitting back against hard plastic. "I know.

You're right. I just hate being away, even for just a couple of days. Don't you think people have been acting weird? I mean, what was up with that shifter on Main Street? I've never seen one act like that."

Jasmin didn't speak but slowed down on the chips as she stared at the crowd passing by. "I don't know," she finally said, "But you're right. Something has felt off for a while now. But I can't put my finger on it."

"Can we fly?" Torie asked, leaning in close to whisper in her friend's ear.

Jasmin looked around, confused. "Um, yeah. That's what we're doing here. At the airport. Girl, please don't tell me you're about to start acting all loopy too..."

Torie frowned. "What? No, don't be ridiculous. I mean literally. Like in the movies. Maybe with a broom."

Jasmin leaned away from her, opening her eyes wide. "Have you bumped your head? I'll tell you what. I knew a forest witch once who was convinced with the right combination of plants and herbs she could do that. Had a special broom that she talked to and everything. Climbed up on her roof, recited an ancient incantation she found and took off."

Torie's breath caught in her chest. "So, it can be done then?"

Jasmin frowned again. "No, girl, she fell off that roof and broke her back when she landed on a big old rock in front of her house."

Torie huffed. "You could have just said that from the beginning."

Jasmin gave her a slight chuckle. "I know how you are once you start to get an idea in your head. I wanted you to see the full picture."

They sat in silence until it was time to board. Once seated, Torie texted both Fionna and Elric to let them know the flight was underway. She closed her eyes and reached for the wards that protected her home once again.

Elric was more than capable of protecting himself and Leo, but she felt a small measure of relief in knowing there was an added layer of protection around those she loved.

"Ready for this?" Jasmin asked with a smile. "Next stop, the hallowed homeland of our kind."

Torie closed her eyes and inhaled deeply. As much as she wished otherwise, something told her this trip was going to open doors to some very dark places.

Grab your copy...
vinci-books.com/hexfactor

About the Author

M.J. Caan is an avid reader and writer of all things science fiction and fantasy. Author of multiple science fiction and paranormal fantasy series, M.J. likes to think that there is still magic out there in the world. Even if it's only between the pages of a great book.